BURNING
SECRETS

ALSO BY CLARE CHAMBERS:

BRIGHT GIRLS

BURNING SECRETS

Clare Chambers

HarperCollins *Children's Books*

First published in Great Britain in hardback by
HarperCollins *Children's Books* 2011
HarperCollins *Children's Books* is a division of HarperCollins*Publishers* Ltd,
77–85 Fulham Palace Road, Hammersmith, London W6 8JB

The HarperCollins *Children's Books* website is
www.harpercollins.co.uk

1

Copyright © Clare Chambers 2011

ISBN 978-0-00-730728-9

Clare Chambers asserts the moral right to be identified
as the author of the work.

Typeset by Palimpsest Book Production Limited, Falkirk, Stirlingshire
Printed and bound in England by Clays Ltd, St Ives plc

Mixed Sources
Product group from well-managed
forests and other controlled sources
www.fsc.org Cert no. SW-COC-001806
© 1996 Forest Stewardship Council

FSC is a non-profit international organisation established to promote the
responsible management of the world's forests. Products carrying the FSC
label are independently certified to assure consumers that they come
from forests that are managed to meet the social, economic and
ecological needs of present and future generations.

Find out more about HarperCollins and the environment at
www.harpercollins.co.uk/green

To Jules

I FOUND THE bag on the field down by the boundary fence. I was going to take it to lost property, but when I looked inside and saw the name on the books, I picked it up and ran instead. I didn't know what I was going to do – I didn't have a plan. I just knew that it belonged to my enemy and the opportunity was too good to waste.

I didn't stop running until I reached the allotments. It was just starting to get dark and there was no one about. I hid behind a shed, out of the wind, and emptied the bag out on to the floor. There were exercise books, a planner, a ring binder, an iPod and a mobile phone, some make-up and a pencil case covered with biro scribble, a pack of Marlboro Lights and a lighter. It was the lighter that gave me the idea. I had a quick flick through the planner first, to see if there was any mention of me, and I was quite surprised that there wasn't. I don't know what I was expecting – if you were out to get someone you'd hardly write it in your school planner. It made me realise that hating me wasn't something that took up any of her time; it just came as naturally as breathing.

I made a pyramid out of the books, and lit one corner of a cardboard cover, but it didn't catch, so I tore some pages out of the planner and rolled them into a tube and lit that instead. When it was burning nicely I snapped the top off the lighter and tipped the fuel out over the books. When I touched the flame to the fuel-soaked paper it caught straight away with a loud pop. I felt slightly sick. There was no going back now. I'd have to burn everything to ashes, so it would never be found, and she would never know. The books were going well, but I could tell that the fire wasn't hot enough to burn the bag; a big, fake leather sack with loads of buckles and pockets, so I collected up an armful of twigs and dead stuff from the edges of the allotments and threw that on. Then I went to get some more, until I had quite a decent sized pile. The wind was blowing in powerful gusts and the fire tore through the dry wood a bit faster than I expected. It had started to spread out around the base too, and was getting closer to the shed.

The mobile phone suddenly burst into life, flashing and vibrating and getting louder and louder. That freaked me out more than anything, so I chucked it on the fire too, with the bag and the iPod, and all the other bits apart from the Marlboro Lights. I could use them later. I watched the way the white coating on the iPod blistered up like a poppadom and turned black before peeling off. And then the whole pile teetered and slumped against the shed, and I realised that it was still spreading and growing. I started stamping on the bits of burning grass around the edges but I couldn't do anything to stop the wall of fire leaping up the side of the shed.

I looked around for something that I could use to put it out. About fifty metres away there was a stand-pipe tap which gardeners used to water their vegetables, but there was no hose or watering can lying around. I would have rung 999 but I was scared to use my mobile because I'd be in big trouble if someone traced the call, so I ran across the allotments and down the alley to the main road where there was a phone box. And that's when I saw you, strolling back from training with your kitbag on your back. I told you what I'd done and you said, Don't worry, I'll sort it out. Go home, and don't tell anyone what happened. Go on. Run. So that's what I did.

Sorry.

1

APPROXIMATELY HALFWAY BETWEEN the mainland and the island, at the point where neither coast was visible – even on a clear day, which this wasn't – the signal on Daniel's mobile phone faded away, never to reappear.

"Dead," he said, dropping it into the open jaws of his rucksack, and slumping even further down in his seat.

His mum glanced up from her crossword. "I did warn you," she said. "This isn't London."

Louie, lying at full stretch along the padded bench seat, with her head on a balled-up sweater, twitched awake. "How much longer?" she muttered queasily, without opening her eyes.

"An hour and a half," said her mum.

Louie gave a groan and pressed her face, which had taken on the greyish colour of well-chewed gum, deeper into the upholstery.

Although the sea wasn't especially rough, the ferry was only small and was swaying and pitching rhythmically with the swell. The few tables and chairs and the lone metal waste bin in the tiny passenger lounge were bolted to the floor. Daniel watched the blue horizon rise up and almost fill the window, then drop back out of sight again each time the boat rolled. He felt dizzily claustrophobic as he always did when caged in, a tightening in his chest warning him to get outside in the open, fast.

From the car deck a short flight of steps below, came reproachful barking.

"I'm going to take Chet out," said Daniel, standing up with a lurch and clutching the edge of the table as the floor fell away beneath his feet.

His mum slung the car keys across. "Keep a tight hold of him."

Daniel rolled his eyes at this, but she had already gone back to her crossword. As if he would let anything happen to Chet. If he was honest, he loved his dog more than any other living thing. Except Louie, though she could be a royal pain in the arse at times, whereas Chet never ever was. They hadn't had any kind of pets before, not even a hamster, and then suddenly three years ago, this Border Collie pup had arrived – an energetic bundle of black and white fur and razor-sharp teeth – a gift to distract him and Louie from The Divorce. A brilliant idea, and probably the last decision his parents ever made without disagreement. If things had gone a bit wobbly for him and Louie since, they would have been ten times worse without Chet.

There he was now, standing in the front seat of their elderly Vauxhall Estate, forcing the end of his nose through the three-inch gap at the top of the window, his black nostrils twitching in the wind. Daniel staggered across the deck, cannoning between the cars to his left and right, as the boat rode the heaving waves. Chet withdrew his nose, and began capering from seat to seat, barking joyfully at the sight of the lead coiled in Daniel's fist. With some difficulty Daniel got the passenger door open just far enough to admit his arm, and managed to clip the lead on to Chet's collar, keeping the other end wound tightly around his wrist. Together, boy and dog made halting progress up to the passenger deck, keeping away from the outer edge. There was a stiff breeze blowing and they faced into it, whipped by the salty wind for a moment before heading around to the sheltered side of the boat. On the front car deck, which was swilling with water, were a couple of motorbikes chained to blocks. Each time the boat hit a trough another explosion of spray would clatter down on the bikes before streaming over the sides. Daniel's earlier exploration of the boat had taken only a matter of minutes. There were no slot machines, no restaurant, no duty-free shop; just a Ladies and Gents, and a small bar selling tea, coffee and watery hot chocolate in polystyrene cups. A Perspex cabinet on the counter offered a selection of depressing snacks: a solitary scone beside a curl of butter; a slab of fruit cake, sweating in its polythene wrapper, an Eccles cake, whatever that was, and a pasty with something orange oozing from a breach in its pastry wall.

Breakfast – a Full English at the Travelodge in Plymouth – now seemed a long way off, so Daniel bought the pasty. The woman serving behind the counter had microwaved it for two whole minutes so the filling was as hot as magma, and the first bite had stripped a layer off the top of his mouth. He could still feel fronds of skin hanging down like seaweed from the roof of a cave.

There were only three other occupants in the bar; a couple of guys in leather biker gear, who were drinking beer from their own private stash, and a youngish woman with long frizzy hair, who was reading a book. Along with the few people in the lounge that brought the total number of passengers to sixteen.

Revived by the buffeting wind and the reassuring open expanse of sea and sky, Daniel completed his circuit of the boat and lured Chet back into the car with a Bonio. Back in the lounge he found Louie sitting up, rumpled and woozy from sleep, her hair bristling with static and in the foulest of moods.

"I'm dying," she croaked. "I actually am. If anybody's interested."

No one was. Hardly taking her eyes from the crossword, their mum passed across a plastic bag. "If you're going to be sick, use this."

"It's got a whacking great hole in the bottom!" Louie protested, crumpling it into a ball and chucking it back in disgust. It landed on the floor and began slowly to unfurl. Several passengers glanced over, tutting. Louie glared back.

Having failed to arouse any sympathy for her imminent death, she began to hunt in the holdall under the table in search of refreshment.

"Who drank the last Diet Coke?" she demanded.

"You did," said Daniel. "I don't even like the stuff." He couldn't help laughing at her outraged expression.

She was so easy to wind up. He couldn't wait to see her face when she found out there was no mobile reception. That would really cause a meltdown.

Before he had a chance to test this out, Mum was pointing at the window, saying, "I think you can just see it now."

Through the salt-smeared glass, in the grey distance between sea and sky, was a blue shape like the humped back of a partly submerged monster. The Island of Wragge. Daniel felt a fluttering of anticipation in his stomach, like the beating of trapped wings. All their plans and preparations had been based on getting away from their troubles – putting the whole damn thing behind them – but without any clear idea of what they were running towards.

2

*W*ELCOME TO PORT JULIAN, read the sign at the harbour. *TWINNED WITH IVRE-SUR-SEINE AND KRAUSBURG.*

"Surely that would make triplets, not twins," Daniel observed. Another sign showed a cartoon of a smiling sun and a smiling moon above the words *KEEP PORT JULIAN SPECIAL.*

A couple of mail sacks had been slung out on to the quay, and then the six cars, two motorbikes and one lorry which comprised the ferry's entire cargo, rolled down the ramp to form a short queue at an electronic barrier across the road. A man in uniform – some sort of customs official – was checking papers and waving people through. Or not.

Up ahead the two bikers had been pulled over, and seemed to be having some sort of altercation with another official who had emerged from his booth.

"Do we need passports?" Louie asked her mum.

"Of course not. This is part of the UK."

"So what is the purpose of your visit?" the official asked the bikers. "Visiting friends?"

"No. Just a holiday," said the larger of the two, who had removed his helmet, in order to be more clearly understood.

"Where are you staying?"

They pointed to the sausage of rolled canvas that was lashed to the back of one of the motorbikes. "We're camping."

"It's illegal to pitch a tent except on a registered camping site," the official said, as though reciting from a carefully memorised book of by-laws.

"Fine. We'll go to a campsite," said the biker, beginning to lose patience.

"There are no registered camping sites on Wragge,"

said the official with the merest hint of triumph in his voice. "And unfortunately," he consulted his clipboard, "there is only one hotel on Wragge and it's fully booked. August is their busy month."

"So are you saying we can't stay here?" It was beginning to dawn on the two bikers that persistence was not going to prevail.

"What if we *were* coming here to visit friends?" demanded the smaller man. "That would be all right, would it?"

"Oh yes," said the official reasonably. "That would be perfectly all right. But you're not."

The rest of the queue, displaying surprising patience in the face of this hold-up, was eavesdropping shamelessly.

The other biker was beginning to smoulder. He was a big, muscular type, and looked to Daniel like he'd prefer to settle a disagreement with a fist fight rather than a battle of words.

"OK," said his mate, to head off a scene. "What if

we want to have a drive around the island, and then get the last ferry back tonight. That's not illegal, is it?"

"Of course not," said the official, his face wreathed in smiles. "That would be absolutely fine." He gestured to his colleague to raise the barrier.

"What time does the last ferry leave?"

The man drew back a stiff shirt cuff to check his watch. "Forty-five minutes," he said cheerfully. "Starts loading in thirty." He turned his back on their protests, and advanced towards the next car in the queue, beaming with satisfaction. "Welcome to Wragge."

When it came to their turn Daniel felt suddenly anxious that this Little Hitler with his clipboard would find some excuse to send them packing too. But instead he looked over their residency permit and nodded in recognition.

"The Brow," he said, reading the address on the document before passing it back. "Ericsson's old place. That's been empty a while. The neighbours have been keeping an eye on it though. Garden was getting a bit overgrown."

"Well, my grandfather moved into a nursing home on the mainland about a year ago," Daniel's mum replied. "He'd been quite infirm for some time," she added, as though obliged to explain his shortcomings as a gardener.

"Nice old boy. Used to see him walking about in his shorts in all weathers," the official said. "How is he?"

"Dead," said Louie.

"I'm sorry to hear that." The man shook his head sadly. "You moving here for good then?"

"Six months," Daniel's mum explained. "Then we'll see." Daniel knew there was no going back early: they had let their London house to an American academic and his family, and this cottage – The Brow – which Daniel and Louie had never seen, was now their only home.

"You'll probably find," said the official, putting his face very close to the open window and beaming in at

Daniel and Louie, "that once you've settled in here you'll never want to leave."

"He was kind of friendly," said Mum, once they had passed through the barrier and were on their way, leaving the fishing boats and cottages of Port Julian behind.

"I don't call it friendly," sniffed Louie. "I call it freaky." Of the three of them she had been the least enthusiastic about the move, and was ready for any chance to criticise.

Daniel had already proved he could survive without pretty much everything that made life OK. There was nothing this place could throw at him. As long as he had Chet he could be happy anywhere. He wasn't sure about Mum though. Happiness wasn't really her thing. Grim determination was more like it. But Louie was the real difficulty. She felt everything so deeply, and took things so personally – she just didn't have that streak of hardness you need to withstand the knocks. She'd hated school, hated London – but it was difficult to tell which way her mood would swing on the island.

Wragge was only nine miles long and six miles across

at its widest point but the journey to The Brow, on the south-west tip of the island, took half an hour, because Mum took the coast road instead of the more direct route over the moor. The road was narrow and pot-holed, with high hedgerows and few passing places, and they had been stuck for ages behind a woman on horseback, ambling along with no sense of urgency. Eventually they reached a farm gate and she had steered the horse to one side to let them pass, acknowledging them with a twitch of her riding crop and continuing to stare after the car until it was out of sight.

Occasional breaks in the hedgerow gave glimpses on one side of fields studded with sheep, and beyond and below on the other, the beaten metal of the sea. At each junction signposts pointed towards unseen villages with curious names: Stape, Crosskeys, Last. Their destination was Ingle. It hardly seemed to need a name of its own as it consisted of just two houses and a stone chapel, which stood at some distance on a little knoll surrounded by a crumbling wall. The chapel had clearly been derelict for some time as there was a gaping hole in the roof, now an entry point for nesting birds.

The turning to The Brow was indicated by a hand-gouged sign nailed to a fence post, and the track itself was unsurfaced, worn into ridges and furrows by passing tyres. The car bounced along the last half-mile, the suspension almost collapsing under the weight of luggage and passengers, the exhaust pipe clanking each time it hit a ridge. They passed a small boxy brick house beside a well-stocked vegetable garden. A row of massive off-white pants and greying bras had been pegged out on a line strung between two apple trees. Daniel and Louie exchanged looks of mild horror. The front door of the house had been left open, giving it a blank open-mouthed appearance. The empty eyes of the upstairs windows seemed to follow the cloud of dust that marked the car's progress down the parched track.

"The neighbours, I guess," said their mum. Around another bend the road rose sharply, and the car faltered and strained like an elderly cart-horse. Just when it threatened to expire altogether, they found themselves on the edge of the plateau, moorland to their right, and to their left, sheltering behind ivy-covered walls, a simple two-storey stone cottage in an overgrown acre of wildflowers and weeds. The Brow.

3

"THIS IS IT," Mum said, adding, "don't even think about rushing off to explore before we've unloaded this clobber." On closer inspection the garden wasn't all overgrown – someone had attempted to cut the grass, recently too, judging from the pile of fresh clippings beside the wall.

"God knows what sort of state this place is going to be in," Mum said, over her shoulder. She went to put the key in the lock, but at the faintest pressure the door swung open.

Daniel, untying the rope from the roof rack, heard her say, "This is weird." He and Louie left Chet chasing squirrels and caught up with Mum in the kitchen – a large sunny room with yellow curtains and a flagstone floor. It was surprisingly clean and dust-free, cleaner in fact than their house in London ever was. On a long wooden table were three place settings, a teapot wearing a knitted cosy, milk jug, sugar bowl and a large fruit cake covered with a cloth.

"It's like Goldilocks and the Three Bears," said Louie.

"But are we Goldilocks or the bears?" Daniel replied, putting the back of his hand against the spout of the teapot and withdrawing it sharply from the heat.

They moved through the rest of the house, looking for other signs of occupancy, but the rooms, though furnished and free of cobwebs, had an abandoned air. From the garden came the sound of barking. There goes a squirrel, thought Daniel.

"Well, I don't want to sit drinking tea until we've got everything in," Mum decided, heading back outside and almost tripping over a basket of vegetables – runner beans, tomatoes and courgettes – which had materialised on the doorstep, like an offering left at a shrine.

"Coo-ee," said a voice, and a short, very fat woman

in a pair of drawstring shorts, trainers and a man's check shirt appeared around the corner of the house, with an excited Chet capering at her heels. She was carrying a string bag of apples. "Windfalls," she panted, indicating the bag. "Hope you don't mind. They only rot if you leave them." The effort of this act of trespass had left her sweating and short of breath. "I'm Winnie-next-door," she went on. "Been keeping an eye on the place since Mr Ericsson left. I pop in and give it a clean every now and then."

"Thank you," said Mum. "It's certainly very tidy inside. I wasn't expecting that."

"Oh, we all look out for each other here," said Winnie-next-door. "They phoned from Port Julian when the ferry got in. Said you were on your way, so I left you some tea indoors. And there's some veg. I'll send my son, Kenny, round tomorrow with eggs."

"That's very kind of you," said Mum.

Daniel didn't think it was kind. He thought it was creepy having their movements tracked and privacy invaded. This woman wandering in and out and having her own key to the place, like some kind of jailer.

"I suppose you two will be starting at the high school," Winnie said, smiling at Daniel and Louic, who shrugged and refused to be drawn into conversation.

"I'm planning to home educate them, actually," said their mum, coming to the rescue. "We've had bad experiences with schools in the past." Winnie's eyes widened. "Bullying and stuff."

"Well, there's no bullying at Stape High," Winnie insisted. "The head won't allow it. She's turned the place around in the last five years. Got a wonderful atmosphere now. You can tell all the pupils are happy the moment you walk in the place. Oh yes," she gave a satisfied smile, "we're very lucky on Wragge. Our young people never give us any trouble at all."

She set off across the grass, clearly her own short cut that didn't involve using the path or gate.

Fifteen minutes later the luggage was indoors, a small mountain of cases, holdalls and cardboard boxes at the bottom of the stairs. "You can only bring what we can fit in the car," Daniel and Louie had been told back in London. "Which isn't much, so pack wisely." There'd been some disagreement about what items counted as personal belongings and what could be considered 'house stuff' – saucepans, crockery, Chet's basket, Chet himself. Somehow or other – chiefly by overloading the roof rack with larger items and stuffing every cranny of the car with smaller squashable things – life's essentials had been accommodated. Now, they looked at the heap blocking the hallway without enthusiasm. "I suppose I'd better go and get some food before the shops shut," Mum said wearily. "Are you coming?" she asked Louie.

"What's the alternative?"

"Staying here. Putting away." She gave a cardboard box marked KITCHEN STUFF a gentle kick.

"Coming," said Louie.

"What about you?" Daniel's mum asked him.

He grunted, non-committal. He didn't have the slightest intention of doing any more 'putting away'.

From the tiny bathroom window upstairs he had caught a glimpse of sandy beach, and as soon as the others were out of the way he was going to check it out.

"Can we get pizza?" he said to his mum as she shouldered her handbag and made for the car. "Pepperoni."

She hooted with laughter. "You'll be lucky. I'll be amazed if I can get a loaf of bread."

He watched the car disappear up the track in its own dust-ball, then whistled to Chet. The two of them set off across the garden and through a gap where the wall had collapsed, in the direction of the sea. He didn't bother to lock the door – it had been open when they arrived, and the neighbours clearly had a key, anyway. The clouds had broken up and widening gashes of blue appeared. In the sun it was hot after the cool dead air of the house. A narrow path about the width of Chet led through a field of long tussocky grass and thistles to a stile, where it met a wider path following the outline of the coast. Daniel headed in the direction of the beach, picking a broad flat stem of grass and stretching it between his thumbs to make a reed. It gave a piercing whistle when he blew on it.

From the opposite direction, a woman appeared dressed in jogging gear, but striding rather than jogging. She had short dark hair and was about Daniel's mum's age, which meant she was of no interest and could be ignored. Except the footpath wasn't wide enough for them to pass without some acknowledgement. Daniel prepared to plunge into the long grass to avoid conversation, but the woman's friendly smile faded as she approached and she stopped in front of him, puzzled. "I don't know you," she said, which struck Daniel as an odd thing to say. In his experience, knowing random people who passed you in the street was the exception not the rule.

"I thought I knew all the young people," she went on, bending down to make a fuss of Chet, who responded by jumping up and planting his dusty paws on the front of her pale blue jogging pants.

"Oh," Daniel mumbled, tugging Chet away. "We only just arrived." He gestured vaguely in the direction of The Brow, which was out of sight.

"Ah. New boy. That explains it," the woman replied. The puzzled look returned. "I wasn't *expecting* anyone new. My mistake, no doubt. I'll look into it. What's your name?"

"Daniel Milman," said Daniel, uncertain what she meant, but unwilling to ask.

"Daniel. I'm Mrs Ivory, Emma." She held out her hand. Daniel passed his grubby palm surreptitiously across the back of his jeans before shaking. "See you in September, if not before," she said, giving him a last quick smile and what was either a wink or just a twitch, before jogging off. Daniel smiled and nodded politely; it was easier than admitting ignorance. He wasn't comfortable with spontaneous conversations with strangers, but it looked as though he was going to have to get used to it. Everyone on the island was so damn friendly. Or freaky, depending on your point of view. At least she hadn't cringed away from Chet and his dirty paw prints.

A steep flight of wooden steps with a rope handrail led from the cliff top down to the beach. The tide was a long way out, leaving a broad expanse of fine wet sand combed into ripples by the waves, which came rolling in with the full force of the Atlantic behind them.

At the bottom of the steps Daniel produced a whiskery grey tennis ball from his pocket and waved it teasingly above Chet's nose until the dog was nearly frantic with excitement, then hurled it as hard as he could across the sand. Chet took off after it like a hairy rocket. His technique for chasing down a tennis ball involved overtaking it to come at it from the far side as if rounding it up, as though he saw it as some peculiar breed of miniature sheep. Daniel ran with him, infected by Chet's excitement and exhilarated at having the entire beach to himself. He could feel all the tension streaming out of him as he ran. Once he had burned off some pent-up energy, Daniel began to explore the ridge of seaweed at the high-water mark, to see if anything had been washed up. But there was nothing interesting, no jellyfish, no messages in bottles, no litter, no driftwood. The only trace of civilisation was a sign below the crumbling cliffs warning of falling rocks and a rubbish bin from which a piece of red nylon cord trailed. Daniel wasn't in the habit of scavenging in bins, but the flash of red caught his eye. On investigating, he found that the cord was the handle of a blue drawstring bag made of sturdy waterproof canvas. A logo in the corner showed what looked like a curling leaf or possibly a crooked smile. It was brand new and just what he could do with for carrying swimming gear to the beach. Daniel thought it was an odd thing to chuck away. Maybe it had been accidentally left behind by someone, then dumped in the bin by a tidy-minded citizen of Wragge. Still, finders keepers.

Up on the cliff two girls watched the blond-haired boy with the dog running across the sand. "I don't recognise him, do you?" said the older of the two, squinting into the sunset.

"He looks like Alex Lowey," said the younger one without much interest. "But Alex Lowey hasn't got a dog."

"He's way fitter than Alex," the older girl insisted. "He must be new." She absent-mindedly pulled up a leaf from amongst the grass she was lying on, and began to chew it.

"Can we go home now?" her sister asked. "I'm hungry."

"You can. I'm just watching."

"Do you fancy him or something?"

"I can't tell from up here. I wish I had some binoculars."

Back at The Brow Daniel found Mum and Louie had returned from their shopping trip. They had only gone as far as the first village – Crosskeys – which had a small grocer's selling milk, cheese, bread and various tins and packets, but no pizza. That was a pity, as it looked as though he and Louie would be getting their own dinner. Even though it was only six o'clock, Mum had retired to her bedroom – Daniel knew she wouldn't surface until the following morning.

He began to pick unenthusiastically through the tins of soup and beans.

"Get this," said Louie, who had just unpacked their last purchase – the *Wragge Advertiser*, an eight-page newspaper – and was sniggering over the headlines. "*POLICE REPORT THE DISAPPEARANCE OF A MILK BOTTLE FROM OPIE STREET*. My God, it's a crime hot-spot. Where did you get that?" she added, noticing the canvas bag Daniel was holding.

"Found it in a bin." Louie looked sceptical. "I did!" Daniel protested.

"It looks brand new."

"I know. That's why I kept it. I wouldn't pick some manky old thing out of a bin, would I?" He shook his head.

"What about this," Louie said, turning back to the paper. "*TWO CARS INVOLVED IN COLLISION IN PORT JULIAN: NO ONE HURT.*"

Daniel looked over her shoulder. Another headline: *CRASH BANG WALLOP WHAT A STORM!* was accompanied by a photo of a fallen tree lying across the bonnet of a car. The article described the damage wreaked by the tail end of Hurricane Edna. It wasn't a particularly convincing name for a hurricane. Edna brought to mind comfy slippers and false teeth rather than a violent force of nature. He stopped as a different photograph caught his eye. *Students celebrate exam success* ran the caption; *School Principal congratulates pupils of Stape High.* The woman in the picture surrounded by students and smiling confidently into the camera was unmistakably the same person he had just met on the cliff path.

"I know her," he said, plonking a finger on the photo.

"How come?" asked Louie.

"Met her just a minute ago. She never said she was

head of the school." Her remarks made more sense now and left Daniel with an uneasy feeling.

"You don't mean you actually had a conversation with someone?"

"I didn't start it," Daniel admitted. "She thinks we're going to go to the school."

"What?" said Louie, horrified.

"She just assumed it. Never said I would be."

Louie's cheeks flamed red. "There's No Way I'm Going to School." The promise of home education was the only thing that had made her cooperate with this move to the island. Louie would rather hide out on the moors and live in a ditch than set foot in a school again. A wave of sickness rose up and the back of her throat burned. "Mum *promised*."

"Well, that's OK then," said Daniel, a trifle impatiently. "We just keep our heads down, keep out of trouble. How hard can that be?"

4

MUM SEEMED IN no great hurry to begin her home education project, which suited Daniel and Louie just fine. "We need a few days to settle in, get our bearings," she said over 'breakfast' the following afternoon. (None of them were early risers and breakfast was often overtaken by lunch.)

Daniel had spent a restless night, kept awake by the unfamiliar smells and noises of the house and by the unbroken darkness of the countryside. Just before going to bed he had stepped outside to fetch his book from the car and found the garden path swallowed up in blackness. There were no shadows, no shapes; just deep, thick, solid darkness. He'd felt a prickle of fear, much worse than what he sometimes felt on the street in London at night.

There you could see trouble coming. Then, just after midnight, he'd been wrenched awake by a noise from the garden. He lay there, heart hammering, confused by his strange surroundings and unable to work out where he was. For a few terrible moments he thought he was still inside Lissmore, that his release and everything since was just a dream. The idea almost made him cry out in panic. Then the noise came again – an owl screeching in the trees – and he remembered he was at The Brow. Even so, he had to get up and try the door, reassuring himself that he wasn't locked in.

"You might as well go and have a wander," his mum advised, once breakfast/lunch was over. "I've got things to do."

"Are you going to get the computer set up?" Louie asked.

"Well, I'll try and sort something out. I've got to make phone calls," Mum said vaguely.

"I bet there's no internet connection out here in the

back of beyond," said Louie, who hated being offline even for a day. Already Louie had turned on the ancient TV in the living room, and found the screen a blizzard of grey dots. "What the hell's wrong with this thing?" she demanded, thumping the top of the set.

"There's probably no reception," said Mum with the infuriating casualness of someone who doesn't watch TV. Adjusting the aerial had made it slightly worse. The only thing that brought any improvement in picture quality was standing on a particular floorboard by the window, behind the TV.

"Stay there while I watch *Hollyoaks*," Louie instructed Daniel. "Don't move."

"But I can't even see the screen," Daniel protested.

"That's OK. You don't like *Hollyoaks*, anyway."

Another let-down was the piano in the back room. Daniel no longer had lessons because he hated doing grades, but he'd reached a decent standard before quitting. He still liked playing and sometimes, especially if he was feeling stressed or down, he would sit at the piano for an hour or more, picking out a tune that he'd heard on the radio, chord by chord until he had it just right. They couldn't bring the Yamaha from London, but Daniel's mum assured him that there was definitely a piano at The Brow as her grandfather used to play.

He'd tried it out that first evening after their dinner of tinned soup. It looked like a relic from a saloon bar in the Wild West. The wood was warped and stained, as if by generations of spilled beer, and the keys were chipped and yellowish, like witches' teeth. He wouldn't have been surprised to see a few bullet holes in the side. He pressed middle C and it let out a woolly *plunk* and stayed down. Oh well.

Since there was nothing to do indoors, Daniel and Louie agreed to go for a walk. As they left the house a guy of about twenty with shaggy hair and a furtive expression was walking across the grass towards the front door, carrying a cardboard box. "Eggs," he said, thrusting the box into Daniel's arms and lurching off without waiting for a reply.

"Kenny-next-door," Louie said, as he crashed through a gap in the bramble hedge as though being chased by a pack of dogs.

"Thanks," Daniel called after his departing back.

"Do you think he's a bit weird?" Louie asked, without troubling to lower her voice.

"I dunno," muttered Daniel. "Probably." He shook his head. "This place."

"We're going to be all right though, aren't we?" said Louie, looking to him for reassurance.

"Yeah. Course we are. Anyway, it's better than…" He didn't need to finish the sentence. Lissmore was never mentioned. The word was as unspeakable as cancer.

They set off, following the path inland, keeping Chet on the lead in case he started chasing sheep. It was a hot, still day and the sun was pressing down from an empty sky. Louie must be boiling in that sweater, thought Daniel. But she would never wear short sleeves, however hot it was. Another unmentionable. Perhaps if they could find an empty beach like the one yesterday, with no one around, she might be persuaded to put on a swimsuit and go in the sea. She used to like swimming before the business with her arms.

The footpath led them through fields of sugar beet, rapeseed and neatly furrowed soil parcelled up into tidy squares by dense hedgerows, on to the moor. On a distant hill what appeared at first to be a crucified man revealed itself to be a sagging scarecrow guarding a bare unploughed field. Above their heads birds with long forked tails wheeled and soared gracefully.

"What are those birds called?" Louie asked.

"Dunno," said Daniel. "Birds all look the same to me."

After twenty minutes of steady walking the path divided, offering Stape to the left or Darrow to the right. Daniel remembered the name Stape from the previous day and turned automatically left, along a dirt track marked by the imprint of horses' hooves. They wound their way upwards, beating off clouds of midges hovering at face level. From the top of a stile they had a panoramic view of brown moorland criss-crossed by footpaths and one snaking road. Beyond and below the moor lay the village of Stape, dominated by a large brick-and-glass structure that was unmistakably the school. It was surrounded by lush playing fields, on which groups of children appeared to be crawling around as if hunting for something.

"I didn't think term had started," said Daniel.

"Why would anyone go back before they had to?" Louie replied with a shudder. The thought of school, any school, made her queasy. Even the architecture depressed her.

"What are they doing?" Daniel wondered aloud, watching the children foraging. It looked like a fingertip search of a crime scene.

"Perhaps it's some sort of punishment," suggested Louie. "Like litter duty. Perhaps they have to weed the whole field."

They carried on, hot and thirsty by now and hoping that there would be somewhere to buy a drink. They hadn't thought to bring anything, forgetting that unlike London, snacks might not be available on every corner, round the clock. After half an hour they reached the boundary of the school playing field and stopped for a moment to rest. At closer range they could see that the children weren't as young as they'd first supposed, but were mostly teenagers, and were picking leaves from amongst the blades of grass and collecting them in pockets, paper bags or plastic lunchboxes. Those nearest the boundary stopped and glanced up at the newcomers, shielding their eyes against the glare of the sun. This movement triggered a Mexican wave effect around the field, with everyone gradually abandoning what they were doing and kneeling up to get a proper look. Daniel and Louie walked on hurriedly.

Another few minutes brought them to the village itself – a dozen or so houses around a triangular green formed by the convergence of three roads. In the middle of the green was a pond, patrolled by pristine white ducks, and there was outdoor seating – overspill from the café opposite – which was occupied by a group of teenagers drinking coffee and enjoying the last gasps of summer.

Daniel had the sensation of stepping out on stage as he and Louie made their self-conscious way across the green towards the café. Conversation at the tables fell silent as they passed, all eyes following their progress with frank but not unfriendly curiosity. The back of Daniel's neck felt warm and prickly, as though stares of that intensity could actually generate their own heat.

"Do we look like aliens or something?" Louie hissed as they reached the safety of the pavement.

"I don't know whether I feel like a celebrity or a freak," Daniel muttered back, hooking Chet's lead to a bollard and settling him down with a Bonio.

Inside the café was no better. All heads turned as Daniel and Louie hovered in the doorway, uncertain whether to sit and wait to be served or order from the counter. Fortunately the woman behind the till came to their rescue and beckoned them forward. "What can I get you?" she asked, smiling helpfully. There didn't seem to be anything much on display, apart from a modest selection of filled rolls.

"A Diet Coke and a Tango, please," said Daniel, bringing out a handful of change.

The woman sucked in her breath and shook her head as though Daniel had requested some rare and exotic cocktail. "I don't think I've got any of that. Goodness me, *Coca-Cola*. That's a blast from the past. No one's asked me for one of those for a long time."

Daniel and Louie glanced at each other. "Oh, er, well, Sprite, 7-Up, whatever?" Louie suggested.

Again, this drew a blank. Daniel began to wonder if this was a wind-up, a special way of letting strangers know they weren't welcome, but the woman didn't seem hostile. On the contrary she was full of apologies for not stocking what they were after. He glanced around to see what the others in the café were drinking: bottled water, black coffee and glasses of murky-looking lemon squash.

"Water?" Daniel suggested, uncomfortably aware that they were the focus of fascinated attention, and wanting only to get away as quickly as possible.

"Hold on," said the woman, as if struck by inspiration.

"There might be some of that stuff out the back." Before they could protest, she clattered through a curtain of plastic beads and a moment later they could hear the distant sound of furniture removal, crates being dragged across the floor and bottles clanking. Minutes passed, Daniel and Louie's discomfort increasing as whispered conversations struck up at the tables behind them, the words 'new' and 'yesterday' and 'Brow', clearly audible above the murmur.

Beside him he could sense Louie beginning to simmer. She couldn't stand being stared at, whispered about, sniggered over. That sensation of walking into a room and it falling silent because everyone has just been bitching about you. He gave her neck a reassuring squeeze as she bristled.

"Here we are," said a triumphant voice and the woman reappeared brandishing two dusty bottles of budget brand cola, their labels faded to pink. "Found them!" They were warm to the touch and didn't look very appetising, but Daniel didn't want to hurt her feelings by refusing. He held out a palm full of coins, but the woman waved it away. "I won't charge you," she said, "seeing as they're a bit old."

They mumbled their thanks and turned to leave, a dozen or more pairs of eyes boring into them with undisguised curiosity, as they threaded their way between the tables.

At the exit Louie stopped, suddenly made confident by the prospect of their departure. "Do you mind?" she addressed the room. "It is actually quite rude to stare."

Daniel bundled her out of the door on to the pavement, sweating with embarrassment. "What did you want to go and do that for?" he demanded. "Now we'll never be able to go back in there!"

"Like we want to go back to a café that only sells water!" Louie retorted. "Or flat, warm hundred-year-old Coke." She blew the fluff off her bottle and opened the lid – it surrendered its last remaining bubble of gas with a faint sigh. "Oh, gross. I'm not drinking that," she said, pouring it into the gutter. Immediately half a dozen wasps materialised from nowhere.

"She was only trying to be nice."

"I don't like being gawped at," snapped Louie.

"Well, stop being so loud and lairy then," Daniel hissed, bending down to untie Chet. He'd been brought a plastic dish of water and he was drinking noisily.

Daniel looked around for someone to thank, at which point one of the girls drinking coffee at the picnic tables detached herself from the group as if taking up a dare and sauntered over, chewing. She had blonde hair done up in plaits and was wearing a dazzling white shirt and shorts. She had blue eyes and peachy skin, and if she was wearing any make-up it was too subtle for Daniel to notice. She looked – the word leapt to his mind – *clean*.

"Hello," she said, turning from him to Louie as if to share herself out evenly. "You're new, aren't you?"

"We're new to here," Daniel replied.

"I'm Ramsay Arkin," said the girl, holding out a hand to shake.

Daniel tugged her hand with its neat oval fingernails,

so different from Louie's sore nibbled stumps which she was now doing her best to conceal.

"I live over there." She pointed vaguely in the direction they'd come from. "We're having a sort of end-of-the-holidays barbecue tomorrow night. Come if you want."

"Who's we?" asked Daniel.

"A bunch of us from school. That lot." She indicated her friends on the green. "Plus a few others. We'll just cook sausages and play volleyball on the beach. No big deal."

"What beach?" Daniel asked, although he'd already decided he wouldn't go.

"Joff Bay."

Daniel shook his head. "I don't know it."

"Well, you were walking on it yesterday afternoon." She bit her bottom lip to stop herself smiling at this admission.

"Oh." Daniel was taken aback. He tried to remember whether he'd done anything embarrassing, apart from rooting around in a bin. "I never saw you."

"I was up on the cliff with my sister."

"I didn't realise it was called Joff Bay. We only got here—"

"I know. You only got here yesterday. You're from London, and you're staying at The Brow."

"You seem to know a lot about us," Louie said, bridling. "Are we under surveillance?"

She gave a tinkly laugh, revealing teeth stained bright green. Daniel and Louie tried not to look startled. "Oh, it's nothing personal," she said cheerfully. "It's just the Wragge grapevine. I practically know what you had for dinner."

I've got a pretty good idea what you had for lunch, Daniel thought. He'd quite fancied her until he'd seen those teeth.

"Everybody knows everybody's secrets here," she added over her shoulder as she went to rejoin her friends, hips and plaits swinging as she walked.

Daniel and Louie exchanged a look: *you don't know ours*.

"YOU SHOULDN'T BE HERE."

"I know. I'm sorry."

The man sitting on the other side of the desk had my file open in front of him, tilted away so I couldn't read it. He said he was my key worker and told me to call him Alan. I thought it meant he was the one who would lock me in. That's how much I knew.

"I meant you shouldn't be at Lissmore," he said. "It's not for lads like you."

For a second I felt hopeful: maybe they'd changed their minds and would let me go. Then a sudden plunging dread: maybe they were sending me somewhere worse.

"I'm sorry," I said again.

"You've never been in any kind of trouble before this." He read on slowly, shaking his head. "You're not a Lissmore boy," he said.

This was a compliment: they were psychos.

You know that feeling you get when you're coming home on the night bus and someone gets on and comes weaving along the aisle, off his face, looking for a fight? You sit there trying to make yourself *invisible, gazing out of the window as though there's something out there so interesting you hadn't noticed the psychopath on the bus. And you don't dare stand up and go downstairs where it's safer, because the minute you move he'll notice you. The other passengers are doing exactly the same as you: all trying to be invisible, knowing that one of you is going to get your head kicked in and hoping like hell it isn't them. That was the feeling I had at Lissmore. Every day.*

5

"*A*ND IF YOU *come when all the flowers are dying*
        And I am dead, as dead I well may be…"

Fifteen clear soprano voices bounced off the high walls of Stape High's music room and the teacher let her fingers trail across the piano keys, until the singers straggled to a halt. She had never come across a choir with such tuneful voices and yet so little musical sense. They sang as if they were reading out a shopping list. "Could we try that again with a little bit of emotion?" she pleaded. "*Danny Boy* is meant to be a sad song. It's famous for reducing beefy Irishmen to tears. But not the way you're singing it, girls."

In the back row of the choir Ramsay was finding herself distracted by thoughts of another boy. He hadn't turned up to the beach barbecue, which was a shame as she'd worn her new red dress and ended up getting sand and sausage fat on it for nothing. And they'd been back at school for a week now and every day he'd failed to turn up. Ramsay's one tiny criticism of life on Wragge, which was otherwise perfect, was the lack of new faces. It was reassuring to know and be known by everybody on the island, to be safe wherever you went day or night. She hated the way people lived in cities; squashed together in their little boxes, not talking to the neighbours, frightened to go out after dark. But sometimes Ramsay wondered what it would be like to walk into a roomful of strangers: people who hadn't already made up their mind about her because they knew her parents and her grandparents and had watched her grow up. It would be nice, just once in a while, to go to a party and not be absolutely certain that she would know every single person there.

Visitors from the mainland or abroad were a rarity – like her friend Georgie's cousin Josh who came for

Christmas. He had been at all the parties, but she'd hardly spoken to him because he was always surrounded by a crowd of admirers. Although more than once she'd caught him staring at her. Then at the New Year's Eve fireworks at Port Julian she found herself next to him when the countdown to midnight began, and he had grabbed her hand and in the confusion of everyone saying "Happy New Year" and hugging each other he'd pulled her around the back of the war memorial and kissed her. It was the best moment of her life. You could still see the crushed poppies where she'd stumbled and stuck her foot through the wreath. The next day he went back to the mainland and she never saw him again. He'd be eighteen now, she supposed. At university or off travelling somewhere.

As she sang, Ramsay made a mental list of the known facts about the new occupants of The Brow. Their name was Milman. The mum had inherited the cottage from old Mr Ericsson. (She knew this because her dad was Mr Ericsson's solicitor, and had witnessed the will.) There seemed to be no dad around. Someone in the house was an artist, because there was an easel in one of the upstairs windows which wasn't there when Mr Ericsson was alive. Mrs Milman smoked Benson & Hedges and drank Bombay Sapphire Gin and someone in the house was a vegetarian, according to Ellen, who had a Saturday job at the grocer's shop. She'd overheard Kenny the handyman, their nearest neighbour, telling the school cook he'd seen the kitchen light burning through the night – that they sometimes didn't go to bed before 3 a.m. It painted a slightly odd picture of family life that made Ramsay curious to know more.

"But come you back when summer's in the meadow," the choir warbled, mechanically, *"Or when the valley's hushed and white with snow…"*

"You're bringing tears to my eyes, girls," the music teacher called out as she laboured away at the piano, "for all the wrong reasons."

6

OVER THE NEXT few days when he was out walking Chet, Daniel often found himself drawn in the direction of Stape High. He would stand at the edge of the field looking at the rows of silhouetted figures at their desks. It gave him a buzz to be outside and free, while others were stuck inside working. Since Lissmore he couldn't stand being shut in.

If it was break or lunchtime and there were students out on the field then he would walk straight past without slowing down. He didn't like being stared at either.

Sometimes he would see shuttlecocks or basketballs flying to and fro through the high windows of the gym. That wasn't such a good feeling. Sport was one of the things he missed. Louie was no good as an opponent;

she could hardly catch a ball without falling over, and never cared whether she won or lost. Swimming was OK, because you were competing against yourself, but only team games gave you that sense of belonging. Already, the novelty of 'home education' was wearing off, and he was bored with his own company.

Another reason for choosing this route was the possibility of seeing the girl from the café. He hadn't gone to the party on the beach and regretted it almost immediately. Now people would think he was stuck-up or unfriendly or just a recluse, and there would be no more invitations. He kept on looking out for her, although he wasn't sure he would recognise her in a crowd. Her face had become confused in his memory with a girl back in London who used to catch his bus. She was much older and never even glanced at him, but he'd fancied her like crazy. Once, when there were no other spaces upstairs, she'd sat in the empty seat beside him, and immediately turned her back so she could talk to her mates. When she leant forward her T-shirt rode up and he could see the top of her thong showing above the waistband of her jeans. It amazed him that he could find this tiny T-shaped bit of elastic so exciting. Now her face was a blur too, all mixed up with blonde plaits and green teeth.

It was Chet who indirectly brought Daniel into much closer contact with Stape High and its occupants. On one of their walks Daniel had let the dog off the lead as soon as they came down off the moors into the village and Chet had been trotting happily along at his side.

As they passed the boundary of the school grounds Chet's ears pricked up. He had noticed something interesting in the distance – a cat or a squirrel – and before Daniel could grab his collar he took off across the field, straight through the middle of a five-a-side football match, barking joyfully.

"Chet! Come here!" Daniel bellowed, as he chased after the runaway dog, skirting the pitch to avoid the players, who'd abandoned the game and were staring after him. In the classrooms overlooking the field heads turned at the commotion.

Chet vanished around the side of the building, and as Daniel caught up, he was horrified to see the dog bounding in through the automatic sliding doors of the front entrance.

Sweating with embarrassment, Daniel followed, smiling apologetically at the flustered receptionist who had emerged from behind her desk.

"Sorry," said Daniel. "Can I go and get him?" He pointed down the long carpeted corridor leading out of the lobby, from which distant barking was clearly audible.

"Please do," said the receptionist faintly.

"Has somebody lost a dog?" a voice said, and a woman appeared from one of the corridor's many doorways. Although she was smartly dressed in a suit and had her hair twisted up and fastened in a clip, it was unmistakably the same woman he had met on the cliff path. She had one hand hooked under Chet's collar; with the other she was tickling him behind the ears. She didn't seem remotely annoyed. "I thought I recognised those muddy paws," she said, smiling at Daniel. "Hello again."

"Hello," mumbled Daniel, hastily clipping Chet's lead back on. "Sorry. He was chasing something."

"No harm done. It was probably the caretaker's cat. He loves a scrap." She looked at Daniel with interest. "How are you getting on?"

"Er, OK, thanks."

"I've been meaning to call round."

"Oh…" said Daniel without enthusiasm. The last thing they needed was someone pressurising them to come to school.

"I didn't mean an official visit. I was just going to say hello. See how you were getting on."

"We're OK. My mum's teaching us at home, so…" It was difficult to find a way to tell someone to back off that didn't sound rude.

"In that case I won't disturb you," Mrs Ivory said, smoothly. "I only wanted to say that you and your sister are very welcome to come in and use our facilities any time. We've got computers and a swimming pool and a gym and a *lovely* grand piano that doesn't get nearly enough use." She smiled encouragingly, and Daniel wondered how she knew that he had a sister. Information travelled like smoke on a breeze here.

"You mean walk in any time?"

"Well, yes. Although after school hours would probably make more sense. The computers and music room are in use during the day. But we're open until seven on week nights and all day Saturday. We've got the best facilities on Wragge, so the students are often here outside of school hours. Don't feel you can't use the place just because you're not a pupil yet."

Free computers sounded good, Daniel thought. Though the rest of the island must offer zero entertainment if people willingly spent their free time back at school. "So I just turn up. I don't have to let anyone know?"

"You just turn up."

"How do you stop things getting nicked, if people

just wander in and out?" At school in London they'd had security gates and keypads on all the doors – even the teachers had swipe cards to get in – and everything still got nicked, anyway.

She laughed at his pessimism. "Theft isn't really a problem on an island this size. Everyone knows everyone. There's nothing much to steal, and nowhere to dispose of anything stolen. Nobody here bothers to lock their doors."

They were interrupted by hesitant throat-clearing noises from the receptionist. "Emma, there's a Mr Chancellor on the line? Do you want to take it?"

Mrs Ivory said goodbye to Daniel, gave Chet's back a last ruffle, and returned to her office to take the call.

"Do you know who that is?" the receptionist whispered to Daniel. "That's the headteacher – Mrs Ivory." And she gave him a significant look, as though he'd had an audience with the Pope or something, Daniel thought later.

7

DANIEL WASTED NO time in following up Mrs Ivory's suggestion; he was desperate to get on a computer again, since it looked increasingly unlikely that there would ever be an internet connection at The Brow. His mum's efforts to call out an engineer to connect them seemed to have stalled in the face of unexplained delays and hitches.

His plan was to spend an hour or two online, maybe check out the piano, and then do fifty lengths of the pool. Louie refused to come with him; she wouldn't swim in public, anyway, and didn't want to set foot in Stape High. In spite of Daniel's assurances, she was suspicious that Mrs Ivory was trying to lure them back to school.

"Go without me. I'm fine here," she said, without looking at him. She was sitting at her easel, smearing thick daubs of black and blue oil-paint on to a stormy-looking canvas. However they began, most of her paintings ended up looking dark and stormy.

"That's good," he said, nodding at the picture. "What is it?"

Louie gave him a withering look. "It's not meant to *be* anything."

"Oh. Right. Well, it's good, anyway, whatever it is. Or isn't." He was glad he was going out now. It was better to keep your head down when Louie started getting artistic. She'd once taken a bread knife to one of her paintings because it wasn't turning out the way she wanted and slashed the canvas from top to bottom.

Mum was in the kitchen, working at a translation, as he put his head round the door to say goodbye. One end of the table was covered with the pages of a manuscript and her own handwritten notes; the other, with vegetable peelings. A large pan of greenish liquid bubbled and frothed on the hob. Some species of soup for dinner, thought Daniel, making a mental note to buy proper food while he was out.

He stuffed his towel, swimming trunks, goggles and wallet into the drawstring bag with the smiley logo and set off.

It was five-thirty by the time he reached Stape and the students had long gone. The automatic doors swished open to admit Daniel into the empty lobby. At the reception desk the switchboard lights winked unheeded. He began to make his way down the corridors, half expecting someone to challenge him and ask what he was up to. It hadn't occurred to him until now that he wouldn't be able to find his way around. The students would know where the music practice rooms and computers were, but there were no signs or directions to assist a stranger. Daniel wandered past silent classrooms and laboratories releasing the faint scent of sulphur and leaky gas-tap into the corridor. A cleaner appeared from a doorway dragging a squat hoover by its flexible trunk.

"Where's the computer room?" Daniel asked, unable to shake off the feeling that he was an intruder.

He was in the wrong block altogether. The woman gave him directions to a distant corner of the building and went on her way, the hoover following her in fits and starts like a badly behaved pet.

As he walked, Daniel checked out the displays on the walls: one whole board was taken up with students' portraits. The standard was dismal – figure-drawing only one step up from stick-men! Daniel assumed it must be the work of the youngest pupils, but the year group was the same as Louie's. Unbelievable. She'd produced better stuff than this at primary school.

There were half a dozen other students already in the IT suite when Daniel walked in. To his relief they were sitting separately, spread out around the room, and did no more than glance up at him and back to their screens. Individuals were always much less intimidating than a group. Over the hum of computers and the air-conditioning, he could hear the soft rattle of fingers on keyboards; apart from that all was quiet.

Daniel found an empty terminal and followed the onscreen instructions to set up a password. A feeling of warmth and contentment began to steal over him as he logged on to his favourite sites, as if he was a traveller coming in from the cold to find a welcoming fire in the grate. He felt reconnected to the world of online gamers out there. Even somewhere as remote and isolated as Wragge you could still belong.

These elevated thoughts were cut short when Daniel discovered that his subscriptions to *World of Warcraft* and other (inferior) gaming sites had been allowed to lapse. Typical of Mum to overlook the important things, he thought irritably. He tried to log on to Facebook instead, but the computer was achingly slow, and after a wait of five minutes a warning message popped up: access denied. He tried another, and another with the same effect, squirming in his seat and sighing with impatience, striking the keyboard more forcefully than really necessary. Even YouTube was off limits. No one else in the room appeared to be experiencing these frustrations; they were all typing away placidly, doing homework assignments or playing silent arcade games.

Exasperated, Daniel shut down the terminal, snatched up his bag and stalked out, letting the door bang behind him. What a waste of time! What was the point of having whole banks of new computers if you were going to censor every site? Even though he generally spent a sizeable part of each day kicking around trying to find ways to pass the time, Daniel was suddenly furious about a precious hour wasted. He was still fuming when he reached the music room. The door had been left open, thousands of pounds' worth of instruments there for the taking. There was a rack of electric guitars, a couple of saxophones and a whole percussion section including a drum kit. Taking out his frustration on the grand piano he banged out the handful of pieces he knew by heart, his foot pumping at the loud pedal. Gradually, the quality of the piano won him over and he began to calm down. It was a beautiful instrument and made him sound a thousand times better than he really was. He closed his eyes and imagined himself on stage at the Albert Hall or somewhere equally unrealistic. The stillness around him was the audience holding its breath. He hammered out a Rachmaninov prelude, blundering in places, but feeling the music with every fibre of his being. When he opened his eyes he was startled to find that he was no longer alone. A youngish woman had come into the room and was standing listening. She had long bushy hair tied up in a loose ponytail, and looked vaguely familiar, but Daniel was too surprised to recall where he'd seen her.

"Very good," she said, taking her hands out of her pockets and applauding softly. "How come we haven't met before? Whose class are you in?"

"I don't go to school here," Daniel replied, embarrassed. "Mrs Ivory said I could come in and use the piano and stuff."

"I should have guessed you weren't a pupil. No one here plays like that."

"I know. It was rubbish. I haven't played it for ages." He stood up to go.

"It wasn't rubbish."

"It was full of mistakes. I can't play it without the music."

"I can get the music for you, if you like. Anyway, mistakes are OK. You played with real feeling – that's the main thing. I haven't heard anyone do that since I came here. I'm the music teacher by the way, Helen Swift." She held out a dry chapped hand to be shaken.

"Oh. I'm Daniel. Milman," he replied, giving her hand a reluctant tug.

"Who's your piano teacher? Mr Reid?"

"I don't have lessons. I quit ages ago."

"And yet here you are, practising."

"Yeah. Now I don't have to, I want to." What he couldn't tell her was that the urge to play had come back during those endless months at Lissmore, when there was no possibility of playing a piano, when it would in fact have been positively dangerous.

"Didn't I see you on the ferry coming over?" she asked. "Are you not from round here?"

He remembered her now, sitting in the bar, reading. "No. London."

"Me too." It was like a bond between them – fellow strangers in a foreign land. Helen Swift made herself comfortable in the teacher's swivel chair and seemed in no hurry to bring the conversation to an end. "I thought it was almost impossible for outsiders to get a residency permit. I only got one because they couldn't get a music teacher. What brought you here?"

"My great-granddad lived here. He left my mum his cottage when he died. So we're living here for six months. Get away from London and stuff."

"And do you like it? Wragge, I mean?"

"It's OK," said Daniel guardedly. He had learnt that it was generally safer not to reveal too much of your own opinions. "It's a bit kind of… dead."

Helen nodded. "I still can't get used to the fact that the shops all shut at lunchtime on Saturday. Mind you, there's not a lot to buy when they're open."

"You can't even get a Coke," Daniel complained.

"That's true, now you mention it," said Helen, suddenly attentive. "The students love that disgusting bitter lemon stuff. Of course they drink mostly water at school – there are water coolers in the classrooms – and the sixth formers all drink black coffee. But I've never seen anyone drinking Coke."

Daniel felt the conversation had gone on long enough. There were still things he wanted to do before the school closed, so he asked the teacher if she knew where the pool was, and she offered to take him there.

On their way they passed Mrs Ivory going in the opposite direction. She seemed pleased to see that Daniel had taken up her invitation and stopped to chat. "Oh, you've met Miss Swift already. She'll be able to show you around."

"It's a case of the blind leading the blind, I'm afraid,"

Helen replied. "I still get lost several times a day." Daniel noticed that in the head's presence her voice had immediately become more formal and 'proper'.

"It is a bit of a labyrinth," said Mrs Ivory, cheerfully. "Are you going to try our pool?"

"I was going to," said Daniel, patting his swimming bag to show he'd come prepared.

Mrs Ivory's manner changed, as if something important had distracted her. She seemed about to say something, but then thought better of it and walked briskly on.

The music teacher took Daniel all the way to the sports block which housed the pool. "Come and use the piano any time," she said as they parted. "I'll try and dig out that Rachmaninov music for you next time."

There was no one in the reception area, but he could hear the sounds of a basketball game coming from the gym. In the changing room, which smelled powerfully of feet, there were uniforms and kitbags on the benches. He changed quickly into his trunks and stuffed his clothes, towel and wallet into the drawstring bag, which he hung on a peg. He wished he'd thought to bring a drink with him, and then noticed a water cooler in the corner. The clear bluish plastic of the canister made the water look cool and inviting, but there weren't any cups. The dispenser was empty and the bin below was full of used paper cones, but Daniel decided he wasn't thirsty enough to make a habit of fishing stuff out of bins.

The pool was a decent size for a school one – twenty-five metres, with a springboard at the deep end and an area roped off for lane swimming. It looked fairly new too; the chrome handrails were shiny and unscratched and the grouting had that bright whiteness that doesn't last. A group of eleven- or twelve-year-old girls was playing on giant floats in the shallow end, their shouts of laughter bouncing off the tiled walls. Perched on a tall chair and clutching a long pole which ended in a wire loop as though in readiness for an imminent drowning, sat the lifeguard, Kenny-next-door. He gave a grunt of recognition as Daniel approached. It was the first time they had met since he had brought the eggs round. Occasionally Daniel had seen him from his bedroom window, weeding the vegetable patch or picking runner beans, but they hadn't spoken. His mum had decided, in that way she had of instantly judging and labelling people, that he was retarded.

"Hello," said Daniel, hoping to engage Kenny in conversation. It would give him great satisfaction to be able to demolish his mum's prejudice by reporting back that Kenny was completely normal.

"Hello," said Kenny, without making eye contact.

Not retarded, just a bit shy, Daniel thought. He could relate to that. "I didn't know you worked here," he said.

"I'm the assistant caretaker," Kenny replied, with a hint of self-importance. "Mr Fixit. I just do this a couple of evenings because I've got my lifesaving certificate."

"It's a nice pool," said Daniel, snapping on his goggles. He felt a bit self-conscious, especially now that the group of girls was getting out, and he'd be the only one in the water under Kenny's watchful eye.

"Don't all the schools in London have swimming pools then?"

"Hardly any," said Daniel.

This answer seemed to please Kenny. "I thought they would have," he said.

Daniel made his way up to the deep end and dived in, surfacing to find Kenny still talking. "Cat's just had kittens," he was saying. "Your sister could come round and have a look at them if she wants. Before we get rid of them."

Daniel gave a thumbs-up sign, wondering uneasily what form this 'getting rid of' would take, and then began to swim lengths; front crawl, his face well down in the water to discourage further chat. He completed thirty lengths without pauses in record time, aware that Kenny might be wanting to lock up and go home, then hurried into the changing room. He stopped abruptly, looking around in confusion: his bag containing his clothes, wallet and towel had gone.

8

DANIEL STOOD, DRIPPING and shivering on the chilly tiles, staring in disbelief at the empty peg where he'd hung his bag. A quick glance around the changing room confirmed it had well and truly vanished. There were piles of uniform and kit lying around on and under benches, but no sign of his distinctive blue bag. A feeling of panic and rage swept over him and goose pimples sprang up on his bare flesh. *Oh no*, Mrs Ivory had said. *We don't have any stealing here. We're all one big happy family.* And now on his first visit, someone had nicked his stuff. How the hell was he going to get home without clothes?

Cold and frustrated, he marched back to the poolside. "Kenny," he hissed up at the lifeguard dutifully keeping watch over an empty pool, "someone's nicked my stuff."

Kenny looked astonished. "What do you mean?" he said, climbing down from his high chair.

"My bag's gone. I left it in there and it's gone. I haven't got any clothes! Is there any spare kit I can borrow? Or can you phone my mum?" Even as he said this he realised he didn't know the phone number at The Brow.

"I'm not allowed to leave the pool unattended," said Kenny.

"But there's no one in it!" Daniel protested.

Kenny hesitated.

"I'll stay and look after the pool," Daniel pleaded.

"Have you got a lifesaving certificate?" Kenny asked.

Mum was right: he is retarded, thought Daniel. "Look, if anyone comes I'll tell them they can't go in until you get back," he said desperately.

"All right," said Kenny with extreme reluctance. "There might be something in Lost Property you can borrow. What size shoes?"

"Nine," said Daniel, wondering what his mum was going to say when he told her he'd lost his trainers. Not mentioning it wasn't an option as they were the only pair he had. Unobservant as she was, she'd notice if he took to going out without shoes.

After five minutes waiting in the cold, Kenny returned carrying a short green science overall and a pair of rugby boots, thickly crusted with dried mud. "All I could find," he said apologetically, as he handed them over before climbing back on to his high chair.

"Er... thanks," said Daniel, doing his best to hide his dismay. There was no alternative – he had to get home and he couldn't walk over the moors barefoot. The boots at least fitted, although they felt clammy and disgusting without socks. The overall looked plain weird with hairy legs, but it couldn't be helped. Oh well. The locals already thought he was weird – this would just confirm their view. He poked his head out into the corridor, checking that there was no one about, and then crept out, the boot studs clattering on the lino. He hadn't taken more than two steps when the door to the girls' changing room flew open, there was a squeak of surprise and he found himself looking into the astonished face of Ramsay Arkin.

"Ohmygod! It's you," said Ramsay, biting her lip against a laugh as she took in his strange appearance. "Why are you dressed like that? In fact…" She looked more closely at the pattern of chemical stains and scorch marks on the overall. "That's *my* lab coat!"

"Sorry, I was just borrowing it. Someone's nicked my clothes," Daniel tried to explain, beginning to sweat with embarrassment as he recounted the story of the disappearing bag and Kenny's raiding of the lost property box. On any other day he would have been pleased to bump into her – hadn't he kept coming over this way with just that in mind – but not now, when he was looking like a drowned flasher.

Ramsay looked appalled. "Nobody here steals things," she insisted. "There must be a mistake."

"People keep saying that," Daniel said, beginning to get annoyed. "But my stuff didn't walk off by itself."

"I can't believe it," Ramsay said firmly, a frown of concentration crumpling her smooth forehead. She marched past him and pushed her way into the boys' changing room without bothering to knock. Fortunately the basketball teams had already left, although she didn't give the impression that it would have bothered her if they hadn't. Daniel hesitated before following her in, wondering what the hell he would say if anyone walked in on them.

"Here!" she was saying with a triumphant air, holding out a bundle of belongings rolled up in a greyish towel. "Are these yours?"

He could see at a glance that the towel was his. Bewildered, he took the bundle from her; clothes, trainers, wallet, *contents* of wallet – bank card and four ten-pound notes – all untouched. "Yeah, this is it," he said, still mystified. "Where was it?"

"On a bench in the showers. Someone must have moved it for some reason. Is it all there?"

"Well… yes. Apart from the bag, but that doesn't matter." He was so relieved to have his clothes back, and his money, which he'd never expected to see again. Besides, he could hardly kick up a fuss about a bag which he had nicked from a bin in the first place. He felt stupid that he hadn't noticed his stuff on the bench, but there had been lots of other kit lying around then, and he'd been looking for the blue bag rather than its contents.

Ramsay, pleased to have defended the honesty of her fellow students so successfully, was enjoying the double benefit of having been both right and helpful. "No, no, don't thank me, it was a pleasure," she said wryly.

He looked up sharply and saw she was smiling. "Thank you," he said with heavy emphasis. "I was thinking it; I just forgot to say it." He sat down on a bench and pulled off the rugby boots as a preliminary to getting dressed. Was she going to stand there and watch him? "I'm going to get changed," he hinted.

She held out a hand. "I'll have my lab coat back then."

Daniel was surprised and pleased to find Ramsay leaning against the wall waiting for him when he came out, dried and fully clothed, a couple of minutes later. He no longer felt at quite such a disadvantage. They walked out of the school together at a slow stroll towards the village, without actually discussing where they were going.

"You didn't come to the party," said Ramsay. It was a statement of fact rather than a criticism.

"No," he agreed. "I thought I wouldn't know anyone."

"How else are you going to get to know people?"

"Yeah, you're right. Next time I'll come. If you ask me."

"OK. Do you want some Leaf?"

Ramsay produced a crumpled paper bag from her blazer pocket and offered him what looked like a bunch of wilting dandelion leaves. Daniel looked around nervously. Was she really offering him drugs in the middle of Stape in broad daylight? While he hesitated she took a pinch and began to chew them dreamily, a tiny bubble of green liquid frothing at the corner of her mouth.

"What the hell is that stuff?" Daniel asked. In spite of everything he'd seen in Lissmore he was shocked. Ramsay was the last kind of girl you'd expect—

"It's just Leaf," Ramsay protested, taking in his disapproving expression. "It's not a *drug*." She began to laugh at his misunderstanding. "It's just a herb-type thing that grows here in summer. Like rocket or parsley. But it's totally delicious: try some."

Daniel looked doubtful. "It's not hallucinogenic or anything?"

"Of course not! No one here takes drugs." She sounded genuinely offended – just as she had done at the suggestion that someone at school might conceivably steal.

Wondering why on earth he trusted her, Daniel took a small withered leaf from the bag and sniffed it suspiciously. Ramsay folded up laughing. "What is wrong with you? It's like… salad. You do eat salad, don't you?"

"Yeah. But not out of a paper bag. And not for fun," Daniel replied.

Ramsay's laugh rang out again as Daniel put the scrap of foliage in his mouth. A foul bitter flavour like nothing he'd ever tasted exploded on his tongue. It was like sucking an old rusty nail or a leaky battery. "Bleaagh!" he spluttered, spitting the fibrous pulp into the kerb. "That is disgusting." He spat again, and wiped his tongue on the back of his hand. "How can you eat that?"

Ramsay, still chomping away happily, looked at him in amazement. "You are funny," she said, shaking her head. "Don't you like sweet things?"

"That wasn't sweet!" Daniel exclaimed. "It was like… ugh!" Words temporarily failed him. A coppery aftertaste remained in his mouth and his face was screwed up with revulsion.

"Sorry," said Ramsay. "I thought you'd like it. Everyone at school loves the stuff. And the best thing is, it grows wild all over the island – even on the school field. So it's totally free."

"I can honestly say I wouldn't eat that even if I was starving," said Daniel with feeling.

They walked across the village green, past the café where he and Louie had been given the ancient cola. A group of teenagers was sitting on the grass playing cards and passing around a bag of Leaf as though it was full of sweets. They gave Ramsay a wave, which she returned without slowing down.

"Are they your friends?" Daniel asked.

"Everyone's my friend," Ramsay replied, not boastfully, but in a matter-of-fact way. "They'll be talking about us now," she added, when they were out of earshot. "They'll be wondering about you. Wanting to know what you're like."

"What are you going to tell them? What am I like?"

Ramsay met his gaze cleanly without blinking. A tiny current, an invisible spark, arced across the gap between them. "I'm not sure," she said. "I'd have to do more research." He looked away first.

"There are all sorts of rumours flying around," Ramsay went on.

"Like what?" said Daniel in alarm.

"Oh, like you've come here to spy on us."

He almost laughed with relief. "*Spying?* Who for?"

"I don't know. People are saying your mum is writing a book about the island."

"Well, that's not true. She's translating Swedish crime novels."

"Have you read them?"

"No. She'd be a rubbish spy, anyway. She hardly leaves the house."

"Why did you come here? Why don't you come to school?"

Daniel sighed. It wouldn't do any harm to tell her about Louie. Not everything, of course – some things were off limits – but she was so nice, so easy to talk to… "We came for my sister, really. She got bullied a lot so she moved schools, but then she got bullied there too. She seems to attract it, I don't know why. Well, I sort of do. She can't keep her head down and just fit in. She got really depressed and started self-harming and stuff."

· "What do you mean, self-harming?" asked Ramsay, as if such a thing had never reached the peaceful shores of Wragge.

"She used to burn herself with cigarettes. Stub them out on her arms."

"Why on earth would she do that?" said Ramsay.

"I suppose it made her feel better. Or worse. Or both.

I dunno. I don't want you to think she's a total freak. I mean, quite a lot of people do it."

"Not here they don't," said Ramsay.

"You won't tell anybody else this, will you? I shouldn't have said."

"No, of course not."

They had nearly come to the end of the village. The road led away towards Filey, completely the wrong direction for Daniel.

"That's where I live," said Ramsay, pointing towards the last house on the left. It was a two-storey cottage, like The Brow, but larger and in much better condition. A dark-haired boy, not older than Daniel but certainly bigger, was leaning against the wall, bouncing a tennis ball off the crook of his elbow and catching it, over and over. "That's my room," she added unnecessarily, pointing at an upper window surrounded by neatly trimmed creeper. "And this," she said as the boy stood up to meet them, "is my boyfriend James."

"WHAT YOU IN FOR?" said Warren, who had the cell next to mine.

I'd been preparing myself for bare bricks and an iron bed and maybe a bucket in the corner, but it wasn't actually a cell at all. It was a square room with cream walls and a beige carpet, bed, desk, chair, chest of drawers and a thin strip of (locked) window just below the ceiling: a bit like a Travelodge but without the kettle and teabags and stuff. There was a built-in cupboard – you couldn't call it a bathroom – containing a loo and washbasin. I'd stayed in worse places on school trips.

But no school trip ever gave me such a sick dead feeling in the pit of my stomach. They could have done the place up like a five-star hotel and it wouldn't have made any difference. It was the loneliness that was the worst bit. No, the second worst. The worst bit was the company.

"Arson," I mumbled. "And stuff."

Warren nodded, respectfully.

"What about you?"

94

"I didn't do nothing. I was stitched up," said Warren.

Over the course of my stretch I heard this so often I began to wonder if I was the only person in a secure unit who'd ever pleaded guilty.

I was allowed to wear my own clothes and bring a few things to remind me of home. But anything I brought there would end up reminding me of Lissmore for ever after so I kept it to a minimum. I stuck a photo of Chet above my bed and kept one of Louie in my pocket: I didn't want any other inmates defacing it – or even looking at it. I also brought a clock radio, tennis ball, torch, and the sweatband I'd been wearing when we won 56-54 on the last basket of the national basketball finals as the whistle blew. I thought no one would nick a stinking sweatband, but I was wrong.

On the other side was Tyler, or Taylor – I never knew which because I never saw it written down. He was in for nicking cars. He said he'd been doing glue since he was ten, but he'd moved on to harder stuff. He reeled off a long list of substances as though he'd got a degree in chemistry. I'd never even heard of half of them. But his main addiction was stealing cars and crashing them.

Cautions, fines, ASBOs had no effect whatsoever. He had trashed half the cars on his estate in six months, not to mention several gates, walls and lamp-posts. He said his ambition was to nick a Porsche Boxster and drive it the wrong way down a motorway. Then he said, watch out for Roach because he's a psycho.

You're all psychos, I thought.

9

BY FRIDAY LOUIE'S bout of low spirits had lifted and she had finished – or rather abandoned – her stormy painting, so Daniel suggested going into Port Julian to see a film.

Mum said she'd be glad to have them out from under her feet – which made Daniel think of a lump of squashed chewing gum – and offered them a lift into town after lunch. They were to make their own way back by the evening bus, which took a meandering two-hour route along every possible road, or by hitching a lift. Surprisingly hitch-hiking was a common method of transport on Wragge for people of all ages. In a small place where everyone knew each other and petrol was expensive, it made sense to fill up empty spaces in cars, but Daniel and Louie still hadn't got used to the sight of elderly women or girls younger than Louie, standing on lonely stretches of road to flag down passing cars. And their mum hadn't quite plucked up the courage to stop for any of these hitchers – which had done nothing to increase their popularity with the locals.

The cinema was a small 1930s Art Deco building on the corner of Main Street. It was only open on Fridays and Saturdays and had one screen showing a different film each week – often years, occasionally decades, after its original release. Faded posters outside promised that *Jurassic Park* was 'coming soon'.

"Ohmygod," said Louie, folding up with laughter. "That's, like, a hundred years out of date!"

This particular afternoon they were in luck: the film on offer was *The Bourne Identity*, which at least was one that they didn't mind seeing again. They entered the dimly lit lobby that smelled of ancient cigarette smoke and old carpet, and bought their tickets from a plump middle-aged woman behind the counter. She seemed quite excited to have customers. Having served them she scuttled around to the refreshment booth which advertised salted popcorn, vanilla ice cream and inevitably the bitter lemon drink. They felt obliged to buy something since she was standing there so eagerly, so they ordered a vanilla cone each.

"You're the first youngsters to have bought one of these in years," she said, which made Daniel and Louie exchange looks of alarm. Just how old was this stuff going to be exactly? "I'm going to have one myself. And I'll tell you what I do with mine. I dip it in chocolate." She plunged the vanilla cone into a tub of sauce, which set instantly on contact with the cold ice cream to form a hard shell. "Do you want some?"

It looked quite tempting, so Daniel and Louie accepted her offer. "It's nice to see someone eating proper food," she said, taking their money and carefully counting out the change. "Instead of that horrible Leaf."

She ducked out from the refreshment booth and stood in front of them, now in the role of usherette, solemnly tearing their tickets in half before showing them into the vast empty cinema. "Sit anywhere," she said, sweeping her torch over the rows of steeply ranked seats. "And I'll get started. You've got the back row to yourselves," she added, with a suggestive wink which made Daniel and Louie recoil in horror.

The woman was already letting herself through a concealed doorway into the projectionist's room. Daniel and Louie made a point of sitting in the middle of the auditorium, skulking low in their seats, shaking with laughter.

"What would she have done all day if we hadn't shown up?" Louie hissed.

"Just sat there eating ice cream, I guess," said Daniel, and then the safety screen started to rise with a jerking motion, which set them off all over again.

"Do you think she's round the back cranking some huge handle?" he whispered, miming, until Louie had to flap her hand at him to get him to shut up because she was choking on her ice cream.

*

When they emerged into the open air again it was still only mid-afternoon, and the bus didn't leave for another two hours. They'd decided against hitch-hiking: that would involve making polite conversation with a stranger – possibly more than one stranger – all the way home. To kill the remaining time they strolled up Main Street looking in the shop windows. The only other people about on a weekday afternoon were mums with pre-school children or pensioners. It had never really struck Daniel before that the pavements belonged to different groups of people at different times of day.

The shops weren't that different from any other parade in a small country town – and there was nothing much to tempt Daniel or Louie. On the corner of the street was a fish and chip shop called *The Happy Haddock*.

TODAY'S SPECIAL: FISH AND CHIPS

proclaimed a signboard in the window. Daniel had a sudden, powerful craving for chips. He hadn't eaten any takeaway since leaving London, and could almost taste the steaming vinegar and floury potato as he imagined that first bite. But the shop was closed and wouldn't re-open until after their bus had left.

"Why would the haddock be happy?" demanded Louie, a strict vegetarian. "They're murdered, boiled in oil then eaten!"

In the Centennial Gardens – Port Julian's public park of ornamental flower beds and the war memorial – a group of volunteers was building a huge bonfire. The wigwam-shaped structure stood at least ten metres tall and was made of branches, fence panels and other debris presumably brought down by Hurricane Edna, as well as sticks of furniture and other junk donated by local residents.

As Daniel and Louie approached the rope cordon surrounding the pyre they could see broken ladders, banisters, deckchairs and even an old rocking horse which seemed to be rolling its painted eyes in terror at its impending fate.

"Bit early for Guy Fawkes Night, isn't it?" said Daniel. "It's more than a month away."

His remark was overheard by one of the helpers – a man in paint-smeared overalls. "It's not for Guy Fawkes; it's for the 4th of October. You must be new," he added. "Everyone here knows about the 4th of October."

Daniel nodded, wondering how many centuries he would have to live on Wragge before he stopped being considered 'new' by the other inhabitants. He was about to ask what happened on the 4th of October when he was distracted by Louie prodding him in the ribs.

"Isn't that your bag?" she was saying, pointing into the heart of the woodpile. "The one that got nicked."

Daniel followed the angle of her outstretched finger and saw the red nylon cord and blue fabric half buried under a beer crate.

"It looks like it," he agreed. "Doesn't mean it's the actual one though." Even so, if it wasn't his bag, it was an identical one in equally good condition. Why, he wondered, would people keep trying to dispose of perfectly good bags? He was half tempted to climb over the cordon and retrieve it, but tugging it free would probably bring down the entire heap. He tuned back in to Louie's chatter; she was complaining that the ice cream had made her thirsty.

"Let's see if there's anywhere that sells Diet Coke," she suggested. "Isn't there supposed to be a big supermarket? We could stock up."

Daniel asked the man in overalls for directions and he pointed them along the Darrow road. "Huge building," he assured them. "Can't miss it."

After fifteen minutes' walk they reached a small Co-op with parking spaces for twelve cars and wondered whether they'd taken a wrong turning. But it was the island's main supermarket, and there was, of course, no Coke. The detour wasn't entirely wasted: Daniel bought a two-kilo bag of potatoes and a litre of vegetable oil. He was going to have chips tonight no matter what.

*

Back at The Brow Mum had had a successful afternoon absorbed in her translation, which meant she was in a good mood for once, but had forgotten to get anything for dinner.

"Something came through the door for you earlier," she remembered, as they sat at the kitchen table, peeling and chopping the potatoes for a feast of chips. She fetched it from the dresser and handed it over, leaving milky potato fingerprints on the paper.

It was a printed flyer advertising '4th October Celebrations' in Port Julian. *Fireworks! Live Music! Hog Roast! Mulled Wine! Centennial Gardens 7pm. Night Buses will be running.* On the back was a handwritten message.

To Daniel and family,

This is usually fun so come if you can. It gets really crowded, but I'll try to look out for you near the war memorial at seven-ish.

Ramsay.

10

ONE OF DANIEL'S jobs was to take Chet out for his last walk of the day at about 11 p.m. To begin with he'd not ventured further than the end of the garden, using the light from the house as a guide. But now Daniel began to go further afield, armed with a powerful torch. He never met anyone on these walks, and the houses he passed were always in darkness. The islanders had fixed habits and one of these was going to bed early.

The night before the 4th of October celebrations there was a full moon, which by some trick of the atmosphere seemed magnified to twice its normal size and pale orange in colour. It hung above the trees like an unshaded bulb, bathing the landscape in murky light all the way to the horizon. The nights were cold now and already smelled of autumn.

Daniel was drawn, as always, in the direction of Stape. It was a long walk, even in daylight when the going was good, and he'd never made it all the way in the dark. Apart from the distant shushing of the sea and the crunch of their footsteps, all was quiet. Once they were up on to the straightish path across the moor he switched off the torch and let his eyes grow used to the moonlight. Chet had his nose to the ground following scent trails and after a minute or so Daniel could pick out the details in the landscape quite clearly. The moon had risen directly ahead of him, huge and glowing. A belt of wispy cloud had blown across its face and for a moment it looked as though Saturn itself had changed course and come bowling through space towards Earth – making Daniel's heart gallop with a sort of excited dread – and then the cloud dispersed and it was just the cheesy old moon again.

He hadn't planned to walk all the way to Stape, but

there seemed no good reason to stop so he kept going, and eventually they found themselves looking down on the village. He could see the boxy outline of the school; though it was long after midnight, somewhere deep within the building a light was burning. Daniel supposed it was a security guard on patrol, but then almost laughed aloud at the idea of 'security' in a place where nothing was ever locked, and nothing ever stolen. It would have to rank as Most Pointless Job in the World.

He had a sudden image of Kenny with his life-saving certificate, keeping an all-night vigil beside the pool, just in case. However the light wasn't coming from the pool house, but from somewhere in the main block. It was oddly reassuring that Mum was not the only person who worked through the night.

Walking down through the village he took a detour past Ramsay's house. Not for any reason, he told himself, just for somewhere to go. But he couldn't help glancing up at her window as he passed to see if she was still up, and was both relieved and disappointed that she wasn't.

After all, how would he explain skulking under her window in the dead of night? Her curtains were closed and a row of pot plants stood on the sill – a supply of Leaf to see her through winter.

He hurried away, determined to head back home. As they passed the school playing field Chet, who had been keeping close at Daniel's heels for most of the journey, gave a few short barks and took off just as he had during the five-a-side football match. This time, instead of haring across the grass, he vanished around the side of the building towards the car park and tennis courts, still barking. Immediately the light in the building went off.

That's it, pal, fumed Daniel, striding after him. *No more midnight walkies for you. Five minutes in the back garden, a quick pee up against the apple tree and that's your lot.*

He caught up with Chet by the wheelie bins. One of them had been pushed over, spilling its contents, and the dog was growling at some unseen creature which had clearly been enjoying a good forage and was cornered behind the other bins. Daniel clipped Chet's lead on, speaking to him in a low, calm voice, and shone the torch into the shadows. He gave a violent twitch of surprise and nearly dropped the torch. The cone of light had picked out the crouching figure of a woman, who now straightened up, shielding her eyes from the glare. It was Helen Swift, the music teacher. Her face was pale with fright, and it took her slightly longer to recognise Daniel, dazzled as she was by the glare.

"Oh, it's you," she said with relief, pressing a hand against her heart and blowing out a lungful of held-in breath. "Oh, thank God. I thought that dog was going to rip my throat out. Have you got hold of him?"

"Yes."

"Shhh!" Helen hissed urgently. "And turn that thing off!" She pointed at the torch. "What are you doing here, anyway?" she added.

"Walking my dog," he whispered back. "He suddenly shot off so I followed. What are *you* doing?"

Helen raked her fingers through her long hair. "I...

lost a pile of lesson notes today. I thought they might have been thrown away by mistake… so I decided to come and have a quick look."

This was such an incompetent lie Daniel couldn't even be bothered to challenge it. If she wanted to rummage around in wheelie bins at midnight it was her business.

From somewhere on their side of the building came the soft click of a door closing. Daniel felt Helen's hand close tightly round his arm and before he could protest she dragged him back behind the bins. She pressed her other hand over his mouth and made urgent shushing gestures. This woman is weird and crazy, he thought, and was about to shake her off, but the expression in her eyes stopped him. It was a combination of pleading and genuine fear. So he crouched in the darkness over a puddle of foul-smelling ooze leaking from the waste food bin, trying not to breathe and keeping both arms around Chet in an attempt to keep him still and quiet. Over the background rustle of wind in the trees Daniel's straining ears picked out the sound of footsteps and then the distant crump of a car door. He waited tensely for the engine to start, but instead came the crunch of footsteps again, louder as they approached. Something in the lightness of the tread made Daniel sure it was a woman. Helen gave him an agonised look and shrank a little further into the shadows. The footsteps were heading straight towards them.

Chet's ears began to lift and he put his head on one side as he always did when interested in something. Silently, frantically, Daniel stroked the fur at his neck and behind his ears, holding him tightly to mask the scent of the approaching stranger, and praying he wouldn't bark.

The footsteps stopped almost on top of them and there was a creak of resisting plastic as the rubber lid of a bin opened. Something light was dropped inside and then the lid fell back with a soft thud.

Grit crunched under the departing footsteps and Helen's grip on his arm relaxed. The car door opened and closed, and at last the engine began to rumble. Even so, neither of them spoke until the noise of the car had faded out, swallowed up in the dark distance.

"You good dog," were Helen's first words, which almost made Daniel forgive her for being weird and crazy.

"What was that about?" he hissed. "Why are we hiding?"

But she had already jumped up and was rooting in the bin to find whatever had just been discarded. He found her ripping a chunk of card from the side of a stiff cardboard box. Satisfied, she pocketed the fragment, which was roughly the size of a biscuit and had some sort of mark which he couldn't clearly see, before throwing the rest of the box back in the rubbish.

"Sorry," she said at last. "You must wonder what the hell's going on."

"Just slightly." He realised he was still whispering.

"The important thing is not to tell anyone," she said. "I can trust you, can't I?"

"Depends," said Daniel, with scrupulous honesty. Anyone – especially a really untrustworthy person – could say yes to a question like that. "But you can trust me not to tell anyone about tonight. Who am I going to tell, anyway? I hardly know anyone."

"It's too late and cold to stand here talking about this now. Come to the music room after school on Monday and I'll explain everything. No – on second thoughts, better come to my house instead: Wren Cottage on the Filey road. But *promise me* you won't mention this to anyone."

"You hadn't really lost your lesson notes, had you?" Daniel said. "That was bull, wasn't it?"

"Daniel," she said, shaking her head apologetically, "I'm not even really a teacher."

11

LOUIE WAS STILL up when he let himself in. She had been experimenting: her hair, and in addition her ears, forehead, neck and much of her T-shirt were now an uncompromising shade of red.

"You've been ages," she said, curiously.

"We walked miles. It was good, but I'm freezing." He had no trouble keeping his word to Helen. Keeping secrets was something that came naturally to him.

"I thought I'd dye my hair," said Louie, pointing at her head as if he might not have noticed. "Do you like it?"

"Yeah, it's great – if you want to look like Ronald McDonald," said Daniel.

When he awoke it was mid-afternoon and the house was quiet. He found Louie in the sitting room applying a set of extra-long false nails over her bitten ones. She waggled a set of talons at him. "What do you think?"

"Horrible," he said. It wasn't so much the look of them, but their habit of dropping off. They would turn up in the bottom of the bath or stuck to Chet's fur like giant ticks. Either she was doing something wrong or she needed stronger glue. In daylight her hair looked even more alarming, but he didn't risk any more McHair jokes: Louie was quite capable of shaving the whole lot off.

Outside in the garden Mum was splitting logs for the stove, her teeth clenched each time she brought down the axe. Daniel went out and took the axe off her. It was such a simple, brilliant tool – unimproved over thousands of years. The logs fell open like books at its touch. Soon he had amassed a pyramid of neatly split wood; the sight of it reminded him of the bonfire in the Centennial Gardens.

"I'm going to the fireworks at Port Julian tonight," he said. "Can I have some money?"

"Might be some in my purse," his mum said, vaguely. "Is Louie going with you?"

"Don't think so," said Daniel. It was just the sort of thing she'd hate – crowds, strangers, fire – and he didn't really want her hanging around.

"What were you saying about me?" Louie demanded, appearing at the back door.

"Daniel says you're not going to the fireworks tonight," Mum replied, ignoring Daniel's agonised signals.

"Yes I am," said Louie indignantly. She turned on Daniel. "I was invited too."

"I just thought it wasn't your sort of thing," he said.

"Well, being stuck at home bored out of my head isn't exactly my sort of thing either," Louie retorted, planting her hands on her hips. She turned to her mum. "If he's going, I'm going."

"Fine!" said Daniel, bringing the axe down so that the blade sank into the chopping block with a thud.

*

The centre of Port Julian had been closed to traffic for the evening, and the approach roads blocked off with bollards, so Daniel and Louie's mum had to drop them on the edge of the town. She scrabbled in the dashboard compartments for loose change, handing over a fistful of coins with instructions to get something to eat, before driving off.

Even though they were early, there were already crowds of people milling about. Pinpoints of torchlight glimmered in the dusk like fireflies and there was a distant sound of piped music. Daniel and Louie followed the general drift towards the Centennial Gardens, where fireworks were due to take place, followed by the lighting of the bonfire. To Daniel's dismay Louie had decided to cover up her hair with a hat that he'd bought her as a joke present from Camden Market years ago – a flesh-coloured beanie with a Mohican of woolly tufts across the crown. It had looked witty and ironic in London, but here it looked just plain weird.

In the main square there were stalls and mini

fairground rides for children: tiny revolving teacups, a carousel of infant-sized ponies impaled on colourful poles and the tamest set of flying chairs Daniel had ever seen.

A long queue had formed beside a giant hog roast which was sizzling on a spit, filling the air with the smoky smell of scorched meat. A man in a greasy apron was handing out chunks of blistered pork crackling to the people waiting.

Louie was appalled. "Oh my God. You can totally tell that it's a dead pig," she said, pretending to gag. There *was* something slightly tragic about its skewered body and skinny ankles stretched out in the flames, but Daniel joined the queue anyway.

The piped music had given way to a live band on a podium decorated with balloons and bunting. Two elderly violinists and a keyboard player in Stetsons and spangly cowboy gear were playing bluegrass music at furious speed. Louie grimaced. "Why are they in fancy dress?" she sniggered.

Daniel bought a soft floury roll filled with sliced pork and hot apple sauce, and ate it as they walked along. There didn't seem to be a vegetarian equivalent of hog roast, but Louie found a stall selling chestnuts and bought a large bagful, which also served her as a hand-warmer.

Daniel kept glancing at his watch. He wanted to be near the war memorial at seven for Ramsay. Not right next to it as though he was waiting for her or anything, but just keeping it in view. He was half hoping that if he kept his eyes open he might catch sight of Helen Swift. The claim that everybody on Wragge turned up to this event didn't seem to be too much of an exaggeration. It was going to be difficult to move anywhere freely, as more and more people made their way into the Centennial Gardens ready for the fireworks to start.

Suddenly the public address system crackled into life and a woman's voice blasted into the night, welcoming everyone to the 4th of October Celebrations. Looking back towards the podium, Daniel recognised Mrs Ivory talking into a microphone, while officials fiddled with the sound system to adjust the volume.

"I'm very pleased to be opening this event celebrating the life of our founding father Julian Joff Stape, who three hundred years ago established a small community on this wonderful island that we call home." Some applause and patriotic whooping followed this remark. Mrs Ivory allowed it to die away before carrying on. "You know, we are very fortunate here, very fortunate indeed. There may not be many of us, but we have a strong sense of community. We are all neighbours; our elderly people are respected; our young people are happy and safe; we appreciate our environment and look after it; we all have a job to do and a part to play. We have a lifestyle that is the envy of the outside world." There was more whooping and whistling.

Is that really true? Daniel wondered. *Does the outside world care or know anything about Wragge?* Until he came here he had never even heard of the place.

He tuned back in to hear Mrs Ivory say, "What we

have is very special. But you know, wherever something exists that is good and precious and special, there are outside forces bent on destroying it." The crowd quietened. "I am telling you that there are those who would like to ruin what we have here. They are jealous of our success and they want us to fail. But we must be vigilant, and together we can resist these outside forces – for the sake of our young people, and Julian Joff Stape, whose life we celebrate tonight with this terrific display of light and noise! Enjoy the fireworks!"

This speech was greeted with a storm of applause, and then the first rocket tore into the sky and peeled open with a fizz and a crackle, leaving a shower of glitter trails against the blackness. "Ooh," sighed the spectators in unison, as each firework went up, and then, "Ah!" as it disintegrated.

"What was that all about?" Daniel asked Louie. "What did she mean?"

"I dunno, I wasn't listening," said Louie. She was concentrating on trying to get the peel off a chestnut without losing a fingernail.

It was the expression 'outside forces' that made Daniel uneasy. Weren't they always being reminded that they were outsiders? But they were no threat to anyone on Wragge, or anywhere else. He couldn't imagine anyone less likely than his family to interfere in other people's business. Keeping themselves to themselves was practically a religion. Perhaps Mrs Ivory envisaged some form of invasion by a foreign power. *Ridiculous.* Then a sudden memory of Helen Swift's anxious, stricken face rose up before him. Maybe she too had some inkling of a threat to the community? Impatiently, Daniel scanned the spectators, trying to pick her out, but it was too dark and most people had their faces turned upwards to watch the fireworks.

There was a dazzling flash as half a kilo of magnesium exploded above their heads and for a moment the Centennial Gardens were lit up. Daniel found himself staring straight at Ramsay, only a few metres away, positioned at a strategic distance from the war memorial. Even in a woolly hat with ear-flaps she managed to look pretty. She was peering impatiently into the crowd just as he had done. He felt his heart give a sudden kick of excitement as he realised that she was just as eager to find him as he'd been to find her.

12

"HE'S NOT GOING to turn up," said Fay. "I knew he wouldn't."

"He might just be late," said Ramsay, who refused to be pessimistic so early in the evening. "It wasn't a firm arrangement." She had made so many preparations for tonight: making sure her favourite jeans and top were clean, even though they could hardly be seen under her coat and boots, and doing her hair up in a new way to survive the ravages of her hat. Remembering that he didn't like or approve of Leaf, she'd left her supply at home and cleaned any traces of green from her teeth before doing her make-up. And, most difficult of all, she had managed to give her mates the slip earlier in the evening, in case they scared him off. She'd read in a magazine that boys were especially put off by giggling. On reading this she had resolved never to giggle again. Although laughing at a boy's jokes was allowed – in fact, recommended.

As seven o'clock approached, she found a suitable spot to stake out the war memorial. Ramsay had hardly been aware of the music or Mrs Ivory's speech and now the deadline had passed, time seemed to speed up. With each minute it seemed less likely that Daniel would show up and Ramsay began to wonder if he'd ever received the flyer she'd posted through the door of The Brow. Perhaps it was mistaken for a piece of junk mail and binned unread or maybe chewed up by the dog. She regretted the attack of shyness that had stopped her ringing the doorbell and making the invitation in person.

Then in the dazzle of a brilliant white firework, Ramsay had the odd prickling sensation of being stared at. She turned and there he was; for a second their eyes locked and then they were plunged into darkness again. *I knew you'd come*, she thought, her doubts forgotten, blown away by the energy that seemed to stream from him.

"Hello," Ramsay said, as he approached, shouldering his way through the crowd. "You decided to come then."

He smiled. "Of course."

"This is my sister, Fay," said Ramsay. "She's been dying to meet you."

Daniel introduced Louie, who was hanging back in the shadows. Remembering what he'd told her, Ramsay took pains to be friendly and welcoming, complimenting Louie on her interesting hat and her nails, which were looking a bit sooty after their tussles with the chestnuts. She had told Fay to be especially nice to Louie, but not why. Her sister needed no encouragement. The opportunity to make a New Best Friend before anyone else collared her didn't arise very often and Fay had no intention of wasting it. They stood together watching the fireworks for a while and sharing the last of the chestnuts, then Fay noticed some people in the crowd with glow-sticks. "Oh, I want one of those!" she said.

"They always have them here!" She went off to find whoever was selling them, dragging Louie along with her.

"It'd be good if they became mates," Ramsay observed.

Daniel looked at her in surprise. "You read my mind. I was just thinking the same thing. She seems nice, your sister. Do you get on well?"

"Of course," Ramsay said. "Why wouldn't we?"

"A lot of sisters are always arguing and winding each other up. I mean, me and Louie get on pretty well most of the time. But when she gets into one of her moods, it really kicks off."

"I suppose we're just not very moody people," Ramsay said. She smiled, showing white leafless teeth. "I couldn't sleep last night." Something had disturbed her and then she had lain awake for hours, anticipating tonight and worrying that he wouldn't turn up.

"Neither could I," said Daniel. "In fact... I was walking past your house at about two in the morning."

"Really?" said Ramsay in surprise.

"I took Chet out for a walk, and I just kind of kept walking."

"All the way to Stape? At two o'clock in the morning?" It was about that time that she'd woken up; she wondered if it could have been his presence that was the cause.

Daniel nodded. "I like going out when everyone else is in bed. You feel like you're the only person left alive."

"You're strange," said Ramsay, pretending disapproval she didn't really feel. It was his strangeness that was so attractive.

"You said that last time!" Daniel protested.

"We've only met twice and I'm already repeating myself," Ramsay sighed, shaking her head in dismay.

"Three times," Daniel corrected her. "We've met three times." He stopped, as if he had betrayed himself with this remark, but they were distracted from any awkwardness by a huge eruption of noise and colour overhead that signalled the end of the fireworks.

There was a smattering of applause and then the

crowd began to disperse in the direction of the giant bonfire which was about to be lit.

A few people nodded at Ramsay as they passed, and one woman, who was being pulled along by a large mongrel, and obviously hadn't looked too closely, said, "Hello Ramsay, hello James," and was dragged off by the dog before they could correct her.

Daniel gave Ramsay a sidelong look.

"That was my neighbour," she said with an embarrassed laugh. "She is a bit blind."

"Where is James, anyway?" Daniel asked.

"Oh, I don't know. Somewhere about, I expect," said Ramsay vaguely. She wasn't sure how to mention that she and James had broken up, without making it screamingly obvious that she wanted Daniel to know she was Very Much Available. "I haven't seen him much lately," she added, hoping that this was a broad enough hint.

Daniel seemed to be looking out for someone – for James perhaps, or Louie, or just someone more interesting, Ramsay thought with dismay. "I could introduce you to some people if you want," she offered, brightly, remembering that this was the original purpose of the invitation. "Friends of mine. Nice people."

"OK, if you like," said Daniel, "but I'd rather just talk to you."

"Or we could go and watch the bonfire?" Ramsay suggested, backtracking. She didn't really want to share him unless she had to.

"Bonfire sounds good," he said.

But before they had gone more than a few steps they were waylaid by a bunch of Ramsay's friends. They were wearing rows of fluorescent glow-sticks around their wrists and ankles. Ramsay hoped they weren't going to start giggling.

"This is Daniel," she said, running through the register for his benefit; "Amy, Ellen, Rebecca, Sian." His gaze flickered momentarily over the faces of the girls as they greeted him, and came to rest on Ramsay with an intensity that made her blush.

There seemed to be some delay with the bonfire;

someone had left the taper on the grass and it was now damp and refusing to light. Cigarette lighters were offered and refused by the official in charge, and there was some slow handclapping from some of the crowd. At last a long spill made of rolled newspaper was produced, and its flame was held against the meths-soaked rag protruding from the base of the pyre.

They watched, mesmerised, as the bluish flame travelled along the rag and gradually the balled-up paper and twigs inside the wigwam of planks began to catch. Within thirty seconds the base of the bonfire was ablaze, fanned by a gusty wind, and flames were darting and leaping almost halfway up the structure.

"I like watching fire," Ramsay said dreamily.

"I saw James with Grace earlier," said Amy casually, and Ramsay felt Daniel grow suddenly attentive.

"Are they going out now?" asked Rebecca, turning to Ramsay for confirmation.

"Certainly looked like it from where I was standing," Amy replied.

"I didn't even know you two had split up," said Ellen.

"Forgot to mention it," said Ramsay, grateful to Amy for bringing up the matter in Daniel's hearing. "I think they're very well suited." She didn't feel a grain of possessiveness about James. The sooner he got a new girlfriend the freer she'd be.

The burning woodpile creaked and shifted, collapsing gradually as kitchen chairs and ladders and fence panels and the frightened-looking rocking horse were consumed in the flames. The wind changed direction, sending dense billows of smoke into their section of the crowd. They backed away, spluttering and covering their streaming eyes. Sparks rained down, and above their heads shreds of blackened paper danced in the night sky.

Watching the fire, Daniel was hit with a sudden panic. "Oh my God. Where's Louie?" he said, looking around wildly.

Through the smoke and commotion they saw Fay pushing through the crowd towards them. "Daniel! You better come. Something's happened."

13

"WE WERE WATCHING the bonfire and she suddenly went really strange," Fay explained breathlessly, as they hurried through the gardens towards the town square, where Louie had last been seen heading at a run.

"Strange like what?" Daniel asked, his heart thudding in protest. It was his fault: he should have been keeping an eye on her. *A bonfire of all things.*

"Her eyes were watering. I thought it was the smoke, but then I realised she was *crying.*" There was more than a hint of embarrassment in Fay's voice, as though she had caught Louie dribbling or wetting her knickers. "I asked her what was wrong and she said, 'I can't breathe, I've got to get away,' and started shoving past people.

Then she just ran right out of the park. I couldn't keep up with her."

"You didn't say anything that upset her?" Ramsay asked.

"Of course not," Fay insisted. "We were getting on OK, I thought." She added, "I gave her some Leaf and she said it was disgusting and spat it into a tissue – but that was ages before."

They finally reached the gates of the Centennial Gardens; beyond, the town square was lit up by colourful lanterns on every stall and the moving shapes of fluorescent glow-sticks. Manically cheerful Wurlitzer music was piping out of the speakers.

"So she just started crying and then ran off?" said Daniel. This wasn't too bad or unusual. The only problem was how to find her. She'd never get home without him – she didn't have a clue about the buses and would never ask a stranger.

"Yes, crying," said Fay in the same tone of mild disbelief. "Actual tears."

There was no sign of Louie at the chestnut stall or on the benches around the stage or at any of the other places they had stopped. "We could get them to page her over the Tannoy," Ramsay suggested.

Daniel shook his head. "She'd hate that. She'll be hiding away somewhere quiet, away from the noise. She sometimes gets these… er… panic attacks," he said. "Especially in crowds."

After twenty more minutes of searching, they found Louie sitting on a bench inside the beer tent, being comforted by Mrs Ivory. Someone had brought her a drink of hot non-alcoholic punch strongly flavoured with cinnamon and pepper. Daniel would have put money on Louie refusing to touch the stuff, but there she was, clutching the polystyrene cup in her skinny hands and sipping obediently at the dark steaming liquid.

"Sorry," she said, turning a streaky face to Daniel. "I ruined your evening."

"No you never," he said, though he had just been thinking exactly that. He'd have to take her home now, instead of staying here longer with Ramsay. When he'd heard that James was no longer on the scene, the evening suddenly seemed full of promise. But now it was over. And the worst of it was, he should have seen it coming.

"It was that horse in the fire," Louie quavered. "I could see its eyes looking at me while it was burning. It was horrible."

Mrs Ivory gave Louie's shoulder a gentle squeeze with her black-gloved hand. "You felt a bit squished by the crowd, didn't you?" she said kindly. "But the good news is, this is the only night of the year when there's even a chance of finding a crowd on Wragge. So things will only get better."

Louie smiled weakly at this attempt to jolly her up.

"I've said I'll give her a lift home whenever she's ready," Mrs Ivory went on, addressing Daniel. "You too – if you like." Her glance flicked towards Ramsay.

"I'm ready now," said Louie.

"Er... well... thanks," Daniel replied, churning with frustration and buried rage. It was only half past nine. The night had hardly started, but he couldn't let a virtual stranger take Louie home alone – right over to the other side of the island – when she was in a state. It wasn't the first sacrifice he'd made for his sister, and he didn't suppose it would be the last, but for some reason he was pierced by the unfairness of it.

"OK, I'll come," he said, bitterly. Beside him he could sense Ramsay becoming very still.

"You wait here, my lovely," Mrs Ivory instructed Louie, "while I bring the car up to the barrier." She strolled out of the tent in the direction of the car park. Fay, smiling because the crisis was over, sat down alongside Louie. Daniel and Ramsay had been standing by the entrance to the tent during this discussion but now they stepped outside.

Manic fairground music was belting out from the speakers. A woman was walking amongst the crowd with a bunch of lit sparklers, handing them out left and right. It was the usherette from the cinema. Before he could refuse, she had pressed one into Daniel's hand and done the same to Ramsay.

"Well," said Ramsay, to break the silence.

"Sorry I can't stay," said Daniel. They stood there helplessly, hampered in their goodbyes. In spite of themselves, they couldn't quite help wafting the fizzing sparklers around.

"That's OK," said Ramsay lightly. "The best of it's over, really."

No it isn't, thought Daniel. The best was still to come. He had imagined walking her all the way home in the darkness, stopping to kiss her at every gate and stile. His fantasies had taken no account of the distance or Fay or any other obstacle. "I could come back," he said impulsively. "Once I've got Louie home. I'll walk back."

"It's eight miles," Ramsay laughed. "It'll all be finished." She looked at her watch. "Mum and Dad are giving us a lift home at eleven."

Daniel sagged, defeated. If she'd agreed to wait for him he would have run the eight miles, definitely. Across the square he could see Mrs Ivory reversing her car up to the line of traffic cones.

"We'd better go," he said, pulling back the tent flap and beckoning to Louie.

"Call round some time," Ramsay said in a rush, as he turned to leave. "I mean, if you're passing."

"Definitely," said Daniel.

"I mean, any time except two o'clock in the morning," she called after him, in a voice both joking and not.

As Ramsay and Fay headed back up towards the heart of the party, and Louie and Daniel walked down to the car, his sparkler sputtered and died, giving off a gun-powder smell that he would ever after associate with disappointment.

Don't look round, he told himself sternly, and then immediately did exactly that. He was rewarded with a view of Ramsay vanishing into the crowd without a backward glance.

ALAN SHOWED ME the rec room. We could use it during supervised free time. There was an ancient TV and PlayStation 2 bolted to metal brackets high on the wall; a pool table with a foot-long gash in the baize; an exercise bike and table football. All loose bits of equipment – cues, balls, remote handsets and the lame selection of PS2 games – were kept locked away in the office and had to be signed in and out. I wasn't looking forward to being in here with the others when they were armed with pool cues.

Outside there was a yard where you could kick a ball around. It was surrounded by a high wall – not so much to stop you getting out, Alan explained, as to stop people staring in. There was a basketball hoop fixed to the wall, so I asked if there was a ball. Alan didn't think so – Roach had kicked the last one out of the compound. But after tea – the last meal of the day, dished up at five o'clock, so you were starving again by nine – Alan said he'd found one in the office.

The others were crowding around the PlayStation arguing, so I went outside to shoot a few baskets. The ball had been over-pumped and had a sky-high bounce, and the net had been torn off the hoop, but practising shots took my mind off the caged-in *feeling that had built up all day. When I looked at my watch ten minutes had passed – ten minutes of my stretch. Done.*

Then Roach came out. He had a whole bunch of twitches and tics, like all his muscles were jumping. Even if Tyler-or-Taylor hadn't warned me I could see he was someone to avoid. He was the sort of person you'd imagine torturing animals for fun.

But avoiding people isn't an option in a unit of eight. He came and stood against the wall right under the basket, directly in my line of vision.

"Do you want a go?" I said and threw him the ball.

He spun it on his finger, then carefully and deliberately tossed the ball into the air and kicked it as hard and high as he could, so it sailed out of the compound. He smiled and went back indoors.

I shut my eyes and waited for my fists to unclench while red lights flashed behind my eyelids. I began to count down in thirteens from 1000: 987, 974, 961…

I'd sworn to myself: while I was here I wouldn't let anything get to me. No matter what, I wouldn't retaliate or show any emotion. I'd just get through each day 119 times and then it would be over. If I felt myself losing it or welling up, I'd just do hard maths – it's impossible to concentrate on two things at once if one of them is maths.

Back inside everything was quiet: everyone banished to their rooms. Alan was in the rec room sweeping up glass. The argument had escalated – Warren had thrown a snooker ball through the TV screen. The wrecked TV was covered in a blanket, like a parrot's cage.

The night warden had a very deep posh voice. He called out goodnight before locking me in. As the key turned I felt a sudden wave of panic – it was the first time I really understood what I'd done. I had to take deep breaths to stop myself from battering at the door, yelling to be let out. The only way I could stand it was to tell myself the lock was there to keep the other nutters out. But I never got used to it. Not really.

I lay on the bed, listening to the swish of traffic on the bypass. I'd always assumed places like Lissmore would be miles from anywhere, like Dartmoor or Salisbury Plain. But it was slap in the middle of town just off a main road, surrounded by houses, shops, offices. Normal life was carrying on all around us.

I switched on my torch and combed the walls, picking out the photo of Chet as a puppy. My throat burned. 118 days to go.

14

WREN COTTAGE WAS in a Victorian terrace of school housing just beyond the playing fields on the road to Filey. Daniel had passed them on one of his first explorations of Stape, and been struck by the fact that all of the cottages were named after birds.

There was no car outside and no light on; the dark windows had a blank dead-eyed look. Daniel hardly needed to knock to confirm there was no one home, but did anyway, just to be sure. At this pressure the door swung open on the latch. Islanders never locked their doors, but this was taking things to extremes – besides, Helen Swift was a Londoner, and a paranoid one at that.

"Hello," he called uncertainly into the hallway. "Helen?"

Silence.

Stepping into the front garden Daniel peered through the bay window into the room beyond. It was furnished simply, and immaculately tidy. No, not just tidy, Daniel thought, empty. Even his room at Lissmore hadn't been that bare. No pictures on the walls, no ornaments or books on shelves, no possessions, no clutter. Either Helen Swift lived like a monk, or she didn't live here.

Daniel hesitated on the doorstep with a sense of uneasiness, before sheer curiosity forced him inside.

He moved from room to room, tense and fearful, bracing himself for a shock. At the back of his mind lurked the morbid fear prompted by half-remembered films that he was going to stumble across Helen's body, bludgeoned to death or hanging from a rafter. But the house revealed no horrors, only signs of abandonment. In the upstairs bedroom the wardrobe stood open and empty, the bed stripped of sheets. There were balled-up tissues in the bin and cotton-wool pads smeared with make-up. On the back of the door hung a silver tasselled scarf which Daniel remembered Helen had been wearing in the music room at their first meeting. There were no personal belongings in the bathroom, but there was water in the shower tray and dried blobs of toothpaste in the washbasin.

Downstairs in the kitchen were more signs of recent habitation – a sink full of unwashed dishes, half a bottle of milk and a withered lettuce in the fridge. His anxiety had passed, but now he was left with questions unanswered, and no real idea what to do next.

He had to pass by the school on his way home, so he decided to try the music room, just in case he'd misunderstood Helen's instructions. He slipped in through the unmanned reception area, and made his way down the quiet corridors. The room was much tidier than last time, the tables cleared and books and instruments stacked in the cupboards. Through the windows he could see a hockey game taking place on the floodlit all-weather pitch. Dark clouds were rolling in from the west and a few raindrops streaked the glass.

He'd not been there more than a minute when he heard brisk female footsteps approaching. *At last*, he thought, standing up – he wasn't leaving without a full explanation.

Mrs Ivory put her head around the door and gave a start of surprise to see Daniel. "Oh," she said. "You made me jump."

"Sorry," said Daniel. "I was… just waiting for Miss Swift. For a piano lesson," he added.

"Oh?" Mrs Ivory raised a neat eyebrow. "When was that arranged?"

"Last week?" said Daniel.

"Ah. Well, you're not the only one looking for her. But unfortunately she seems to have gone in rather a hurry."

"Gone?"

"Left the island. She was on the lunchtime ferry."

"Oh," said Daniel, frowning. "Is she coming back?"

"Apparently not. We've been left in the lurch, as they say." Mrs Ivory gave him a palms-up shrug. "She didn't mention anything to you about leaving?" she asked as an afterthought.

"No," Daniel replied. For a moment he considered telling Mrs Ivory what Helen had told him about not really being a teacher. Mrs Ivory had been kind to Louie, and seemed altogether more rational and reliable than Helen. Yet for some reason he kept quiet. If Helen had done something criminal, he'd have to come clean eventually, but for now he preferred to keep his secrets to himself.

"Well, I'll have to start looking for another music teacher. What a pity. I thought she was a real find." At the door she turned. "How's your lovely sister, by the way? She seemed such a troubled soul."

"Oh, she's OK," Daniel mumbled. He wasn't going to start blabbing about Louie's problems to Mrs Ivory.

"There must be something we can do for her. It's a pity she doesn't come over to the school sometimes."

Daniel shrugged, refusing to be drawn into a discussion about their lack of schooling.

"Is there something she particularly misses from home?"

Daniel shook his head and then remembered. "Diet Coke," he said with a grin. "She misses her Diet Coke."

Mrs Ivory wrinkled her nose. "Well, it wouldn't be my choice, but I'll see what I can do."

She left him puzzling over the mysterious departure of Helen Swift. Surely she could have left some kind of message? He had been in all morning: she could have called at The Brow on her way to the ferry – it was a bit of a detour, but she owed him that at least.

Outside the rain had stopped and there was a break in the clouds before the next storm came across. If he ran all the way home he might just avoid a soaking. At the door he gave a last backward glance at the empty music room, and stopped as something caught his eye. On the piano a piece of new sheet music had been left out on the stand. It was the Rachmaninov prelude Helen had heard him trying to play from memory the first time they had met. Perhaps she'd left it out for him. It wouldn't be much use to her if she'd really gone for good, he reasoned, so he might as well take it. As he picked it up something slipped from between the pages and on to the floor. A piece of cardboard about the size of a biscuit, roughly torn from a box – the same piece, Daniel was sure, that Helen had taken from the wheelie bin. On one side was a handwritten mobile phone number, on the other, a printed logo. It had been too dark that night to see the logo properly but now he recognised it: a crooked smile. Just like the one on the blue drawstring bag.

15

I T DIDN'T TAKE long for news of Helen Swift's hasty departure to spread. Islanders seemed to feel that it was their duty to pass on any piece of fresh gossip to as many people as possible. Once a rumour was in circulation it was impossible to halt its progress. Only Louie and Mum, isolated at The Brow, remained cut off from this network.

There was no shortage of theories: she had assaulted a student and been suspended; she was an illegal immigrant working without a permit; she'd had a nervous breakdown; she was an outsider, and outsiders never last.

All these suggestions were the subject of discussion at the Arkins' dinner table.

"Perhaps she's got a boyfriend back home in London and she's missing him," said Ramsay, twirling spaghetti round her fork. It was two days since the fireworks and Daniel still hadn't called round. She'd waited in all day Sunday, not daring to go out in case she missed him, and had come rushing home from school today. But Fay, who had been playing hockey, said she thought she'd seen him in the music block. So he'd been in the neighbourhood and hadn't bothered to call. It was almost enough to put Ramsay off her dinner, if only spaghetti carbonara wasn't her favourite meal and she wasn't starving.

"Well, I don't think she's done anything illegal. I thought she was really nice," said Fay, "even if she was a bit mean about our singing."

"I wonder what will happen about the Christmas concert?" said Ramsay.

"Oh, I expect someone will step in," said her mum, grating parmesan over her pasta. "The problem is, there aren't enough of us islanders with qualifications to do all the jobs, so they bring these outsiders over and they don't fit in."

"I don't think outsiders are that different from us, really," said Ramsay, yet at a deeper instinctive level she doubted it. Daniel, for instance. The way he lived was so impulsive and free. And Louie, with her manic tears, self-harming and God knows what else was like no one you'd ever meet on Wragge.

"Speaking of outsiders," said Mr Arkin, who had not contributed to the previous debate, "I found out something about those new people at The Brow today, which makes you wonder whether the residency office does even the most basic checks before handing out permits."

Everyone looked up from their plates, Ramsay a little more quickly than the rest.

"You learn all sorts of interesting things reading old court reports," Mr Arkin went on, helping himself to salad with a pair of tongs like giant tweezers.

"Wasn't it the boy from The Brow who took you to the fireworks?" Mrs Arkin asked Ramsay.

"He didn't take me. I just met him there. With a load of other people," Ramsay replied, a little defensively.

"You're not seeing him, are you?" asked her father, chasing a slippery tomato around the salad bowl with the tongs.

"I don't know. No, I'm not *seeing* him," Ramsay said, hoping that Daniel wouldn't choose this particular moment to call round. "He's actually really nice."

"And his sister's nice too. When she's not freaking out," Fay added, not particularly helpfully.

"Did he tell you anything about his past? What he did before he came here?" Mr Arkin enquired.

"Yes," said Ramsay instinctively, feeling that he must have done. But now she'd come to think about it she couldn't remember a thing he'd told her about himself, except that he'd stood outside their house at two in the morning. She could hardly admit that. "Um, no."

"This really nice boy didn't mention that he'd spent four months in a secure unit for young offenders?"

Ramsay shook her head in denial. She wished she

could think of some evidence to disprove it, but she knew it was true. She recalled those little snippets of conversation that she'd forgotten – that he'd missed too much school last year to take exams; that he couldn't bear to be cooped up inside any more.

"What's he supposed to have done?"

"Set fire to a building," said Mr Arkin. "Burned a man to death."

"How many fires have you started?" Alan asked me. "Roughly?"

"None. I mean apart from the shed."

"Interesting," said Alan, turning the pages of my file. "Because it says in the transcript of the trial: Prosecution: Why did you set fire to the shed?

Defendant: I didn't set fire to the shed. I lit a little bonfire behind the shed, and the shed caught fire by accident.

Prosecutor: Why did you light 'a little bonfire'?

Defendant – *that's you* – Because I like lighting fires.*"*
Alan looked up. "You like lighting fires, but until this point you'd never actually lit any fires. So how did you know you liked it?"

"I don't remember saying that."

"It's down here in black and white."

"I must've said it then. They ask so many questions that are almost the same – after a while you can't remember what you said."

"Does the name Sidney Robsart mean anything to you?"

I wasn't expecting that. Blood rushed to my face. "I know who he is. Was." Even when I'm ninety and so senile I can't remember my own name I won't be able to forget Sidney Robsart. It's always at night when I'm dropping off to sleep that I think about him. I can hear his fists on the wooden door and his dog howling.

The old woman who came to do the allotment had brought a new padlock with her that day – she was fed up with kids using her shed as a shelter, leaving fag ends and takeaway cartons all over the floor. It never crossed her mind that a tramp might have crept inside out of the wind to curl up with his dog and a bottle of cider and fallen asleep.

The weird thing is, in my dream I'm always the one inside the shed. Trying to get out, throwing myself against the locked door, while the smoke and flames rise up and choke me.

16

D ANIEL SAT IN the doctor's waiting room at Darrow, reading the health notices on the opposite wall: *Incontinent? Don't suffer in silence. Meningitis: Know the Signs. Smoking: We Can Help You Quit.* His mum warned him never to touch the magazines at a GP's surgery as they were riddled with germs from the unwashed hands of diseased patients. He wasn't convinced there was much science behind this – surely doctors of all people would be aware of this potential hazard under their noses. Not that there was much to tempt him amongst the decades-old copies of *The Countryman* and *Women's Realm*.

He had woken up with a raging sore throat, as if he'd swallowed acid, and when Mum had peered into his mouth using a pen torch and a ruler to hold his tongue flat he'd nearly gagged. She decided that he needed antibiotics and had made him an appointment for that afternoon. She'd even gone as far as giving him a lift to the surgery, though her tender care didn't extend to waiting around for the return trip.

Several times during the morning Daniel had picked up the mysterious fragment of cardboard and wondered if Helen had left it for him deliberately, and if so why. He'd shown the logo to Louie without explaining its origin, and she had recognised it as the one on his drawstring bag, but didn't know what it stood for. It was pointless asking Mum; she wouldn't know the difference between a BMW badge and a hot cross bun.

The waiting room was starting to fill up with mums and babies, arriving for a weighing clinic. They all seemed to know each other and Daniel's head was ringing with the babble of female voices, all talking at once above a background of wailing babies. Suddenly he felt grateful he was male.

The doctor was a jowly-faced man with a bald head

but plenty of hair emerging from ears and nostrils by way of compensation. His breath, when he leant towards Daniel to examine his throat, smelled of coffee – stale and foul.

"Any earache?" the doctor asked, producing a magnifying torch and forcing the funnel-shaped point into Daniel's ear.

"Ow. No."

"Any fever?"

"Don't think so."

"Not allergic to penicillin, are you?"

"No."

The doctor turned back to his computer terminal and pecked at the keyboard with one finger. A moment later a green prescription sheet rolled from the printer. "Take one tablet four times a day on an empty stomach," he said as there was a tap at the door and the receptionist appeared, carrying a mug of coffee.

I don't have an empty stomach four times a day, thought Daniel, and then his attention was caught by something that drove all other thoughts out of his head. The mug, which the receptionist had carefully put down on the desk, had a symbol of a crooked smile on the side next to the word: *Narveng*.

"There we are," said the doctor, handing over the prescription. "Make sure you complete the course, even if you feel better." He was too polite to start drinking his coffee in front of a patient, but his hand crept towards the cup in anticipation.

Daniel stood up, hesitating.

"Anything else?" asked the doctor, with a regretful glance at his coffee.

"What's Narveng?"

"Narveng? It's a drug company – like Reckitt or Glaxo. If you've ever had hay fever or a migraine you've probably taken a tablet made by Narveng. Why do you ask?"

"Oh, I just saw that logo the other day and now I've just seen it again on your coffee cup. I wondered what it stood for."

The doctor took this as an excuse to pick up the cup. "The sales reps bring all these freebies with them – mugs, mouse mats, calendars, enough stationery to open a shop. Look." He opened a drawer in his desk to reveal hundreds of cheap plastic biros; the kind that give no pleasure to write with, and yet stubbornly outlast more precious expensive pens.

"Here. Have one." The doctor selected one and passed it over.

"Thanks," said Daniel, putting it in his pocket along with the prescription. He went off with the strange sensation that he had discovered something really important. If only he could work out what it was.

17

THE BUS FROM Darrow passed through Stape on its winding route around the island, so Daniel got out to drop in on Ramsay, just as she had suggested. He'd intended to leave it a bit longer – he didn't want to look too keen, and hadn't forgotten the way she'd walked off without a backward glance – but after three days the urge to see her again overpowered all other considerations. If he looked keen, it was because he was keen: too bad.

He was still some distance away from the house when he caught sight of her in the back garden, and his stomach gave a kick of excitement. She was by the rabbit hutches, putting in fresh straw and bowls of cabbage leaves, and Daniel was sure she'd seen him as she straightened up. But to his surprise, instead of approaching him or responding to his wave she darted back into the house.

Daniel continued up to the front door and rang the bell, reminding himself that girls were strange creatures. Maybe she'd bolted inside to put on make-up or something. Louie, for instance, would never answer the front door with bare feet. Or bare arms, of course.

He waited on the step for a couple of minutes, feeling increasingly uneasy, and then rang again, pressing the bell down for longer than strictly polite. Its trilling echoed through the house: there was no way anyone inside could claim not to have heard it, but still no one came.

Daniel was just turning to leave when he heard movement behind the door, and it opened a fraction. Ramsay stood in the gap, with a troubled frown on her face.

"I can't see you," she said, not quite meeting his eye. "You mustn't come round here again."

"Why not?"

"I'm not allowed. Dad says. You'd better go – he'll be back soon."

"But why? What have I done?" They had been getting on so well at the fireworks, until Louie stuffed things up. And he'd done nothing since that could have upset her. Had he?

She looked at him reproachfully. "Why didn't you tell me you'd been in prison?"

The question came out of nowhere like something solid and knocked him sideways. All he could do was try to recover his breath and blurt out, "It wasn't a prison. Who told you?"

"It's true then," said Ramsay quietly. "You killed a man."

One thing his mum had said through her tears, during those awful months leading up to the trial, came back to him now: *this will follow you for the rest of your life.* She was right. Even on a remote island where you couldn't get broadband or Coke or a takeaway pizza, where they'd barely heard of McDonald's or mobile phones, they'd somehow heard about him.

"It's not the sort of thing you go round telling people," he muttered. "You try to forget about it." Since he had been on Wragge, since he had met Ramsay in fact, he almost had.

"You could have told me."

"So you could have hated me straight away instead of getting to know me first and then hating me?" Daniel retorted.

"I don't hate you." Ramsay glanced anxiously at her watch. "I've got to go. You've got to go, I mean."

A new and terrible thought struck him. If one person on Wragge knew, they all knew. The stares, the whispers, the harassment, everything they thought they'd got away from, would start all over again. It would kill his mum. "I suppose it's all round the island by now. *Everyone knows everyone's secrets here.* You said that the first time we met."

"I haven't told anyone!" Ramsay said, her voice rising with indignation. "And Dad won't."

"Why? What's to stop him?"

"He promised me. As long as I don't see you any more, he'll never tell. That's the deal."

18

"HELLO?"

The voice on the phone was male, unfamiliar.

Daniel resisted the impulse to hang up. "Is Helen there?"

"Who's that?"

So it was her number. "Daniel."

"Hold on." There was the muffling sound of a hand on the receiver, and a moment later Helen's voice, tentative, suspicious. "Daniel? Is that you?"

"Yes. I found this number inside the music so I—"

"Don't say any more," Helen interrupted. "Where are you phoning from?"

"Wragge."

"Yes, yes, but what phone? Can anyone hear you?"

"No. No one's in." Louie and Mum were doing the supermarket run to Port Julian.

"OK. Thanks for ringing. I hoped you'd find the number and put two and two together. In fact I knew you would, you're smart."

"I came to the school like you said, but you'd already gone."

"I'm sorry. I had to get off the island quickly. I couldn't leave you a message because someone else might have found it and I don't want anyone connecting us. I knew no one else would look twice at the sheet music."

"Why mustn't people connect us?"

"Because if they think you're anything to do with me you'll be no use to me."

Daniel wondered when he had agreed to be useful. Chet whisked in from the garden and stood beside Daniel, panting. "Who are 'they'? What's going on? What's Narveng?"

"I can hear breathing," said Helen sharply. "Someone's listening in."

"It's just Chet," laughed Daniel, holding the phone out towards the dog, who sniffed at it then wandered off.

"How do you know about Narveng?" Helen demanded.

"No, you've got to tell me," said Daniel, suddenly impatient, "not the other way round. Why you were hiding behind the bins? What were you looking for and why did you leave? And what did you mean you aren't 'even really a teacher'? I promised not to tell anyone and I haven't. So now you've got to explain."

"Right. Where to start… I'm not a teacher, I'm a journalist. I did a degree in music and drama, even worked at a school for a term after leaving university, but I'm not qualified. I got this job using false references provided by my editor, which is not even vaguely legal. He wanted someone to go undercover to follow up a story that he'd heard about Stape High. But you can't just waltz over from the mainland and start sniffing around the island. You've got to have a residency permit, which means you were either born there or have family there – like your mum – or get a job no one on the island can do. So when the music job came up I applied for it."

"What was the story he'd heard?"

"When you work on a newspaper, you get all sorts of cranks and nutters writing and phoning you with barmy ideas and conspiracy theories – you know: people who think the moon landings never happened and Michael Jackson is still alive. Anyway, one of these calls was from a nurse in a hospice on the mainland. She said that she'd looked after a cancer patient who used to work as a groundsman at Stape High and before he died he told her that 'what's going on at the school is unnatural' and 'one day it will all come out'. She didn't know what he meant at the time, and now he's dead. She was worried though, because she imagined he must have been talking about child abuse. My editor did a bit of his own research about the school, but couldn't find one negative thing about it. In fact, quite the reverse – all evidence was that the children were really happy, placid and well behaved. You've seen what it's like – they even hang out there at weekends and after hours."

"Well, that's 'unnatural' for a start," said Daniel.

"Exactly. So having drawn a blank, my editor just filed it away in the back of his mind. Then six months later he was judging an art prize and got talking to one of the other judges; the subject of Wragge came up. This man and his wife had divorced, partly because of the wild behaviour of their teenage daughter, and the wife had gone back to live on the island, where she'd been born, taking the daughter with her. The man said that within just a few weeks, his daughter completely changed. Instead of having violent mood swings and getting into confrontations with people over nothing, she became a different person – easy-going, cheerful, lovely. From being someone who was always bunking off school, now she was spending all her time there – even weekends and holidays. He thought maybe she'd just grown out of a rebellious phase, but then the next summer holidays she came back to London to spend a month with him. By the third week she had completely reverted to her old ways and they were having screaming, door-slamming rows at three o'clock in the morning. He had to take her back to her mum a week early because he couldn't stand it any more. But as soon as she was back on Wragge she was fine again. He began to wonder if he was the problem. But when he went to visit her on the island, they got along fine – she was a different person. She was 'unnaturally placid', he said, and that got my editor thinking again about what the groundsman had said. Are you still there?"

"Yes, yes," said Daniel, who had been listening out for the car with his free ear. "Carry on."

"Now, here's the funny thing. My editor decided to contact the nurse from the hospice to see if she'd remembered anything more. When he rang the number she'd given him, someone else answered and said she didn't live there any more; she'd come into some money and gone to live in Spain. It took a while to track her down. When he finally got hold of her, she claimed to have no memory of her original call, and denied knowing anything about a groundsman from Stape High. He knew she was lying. And when he rang again a week later the number had been disconnected. So now he really was suspicious: someone was obviously paying her to keep quiet. So I was supposed to get a job at the school and find out what exactly was going on."

"So what were you doing when I found you behind the bins?"

"I'd let myself into the school at night to have a look through the files, but when I arrived there was a light on in the building. I didn't want to bump into anyone, so I hid round the back to wait for whoever it was to leave. Then you and Chet turned up."

"Why did you take something out of the bin?"

"I wondered why someone would dump something in the middle of the night – unless they didn't want anyone else to see them doing it. I wanted to know what it was, but the box was blank apart from that smiley logo, so I tore it off and kept it so I could find out what it stood for, but you already beat me to it."

"Narveng," said Daniel. "Although I don't know much more than that." He explained the various times he'd seen the logo: on his bag he'd found in the bin, the bag on the bonfire, and finally at the doctor's.

"That's three times someone has tried to get rid of something with the Narveng logo," said Helen. "Twice in bins and once by burning. Someone wants to destroy any evidence of a connection between Narveng and the school. So that's the connection we've got to find."

What do you mean, 'we'? thought Daniel, and then his mind took off in another direction. "Why did you run away from the island?"

"I was scared. On the Saturday evening while everyone was at the fireworks I went into school for another look around. When I got back I could tell that an intruder had been in my house. Nothing had been taken, but I knew straight away that things weren't exactly as I'd left them. And there was a strange smell."

"What sort of smell?"

"I don't know. Like chlorine or something. I think they were trying to find out if I really was who I said I was, or if I'd found out anything. And the worst of it? There was no break-in. Someone had a key. That's what really freaked me out. So I packed up to leave. There's no point staying on if the people you're supposed to be spying on know more about you than you do about them. I went into school in the morning to leave you my phone number and there was a note on my desk from Mrs Ivory. It said she'd just had a call from the Education Office about some 'irregularity' with my paperwork, and could I come and see her as a matter of urgency. My cover was completely blown. I couldn't stay and incriminate my editor, so I left on the lunchtime boat."

"Are you planning to come back?"

"I can't. I'd be arrested the moment I stepped off the ferry."

"There must be other ways of getting here. Secretly."

"What – you mean row across the Atlantic? I'm not James Bond."

"Well, how can you find out what's going on here if you're stuck in London?" Daniel asked. Out of the corner of his eye he could see a dust cloud approaching up the lane. In a few moments Mum would be back with the shopping, calling for him to carry the bags from the car.

"I can't," said Helen. "You're going to have to do it for me."

19

O N SATURDAY MORNING Ramsay set off for her job
at the stables at Filey. In exchange for a few
hours' labour mucking out, cleaning tack, feeding and
grooming, she was allowed to take her favourite pony,
Trampus, for a ride along the lanes and, if she was
feeling adventurous, up on to the moors. None of the
stable girls were ever paid for their work, but the privilege
of free rides was enough to ensure that there was no
shortage of volunteers.

As Ramsay left the house, with her riding hat,
containing a packed lunch and an apple for Trampus,
slung over one arm like a basket, she noticed Fay in
the back garden, dusting down their shared bicycle. It
was a while since either of them had used it, as was

evident from its cobwebbed frame and depressed-looking tyres.

"Where are you off to on that thing?" she asked, watching in amusement as Fay wrestled with the pump.

"For a ride over to Ingle," panted Fay, when she had finally managed to force some air into the tyres, satisfied that they weren't punctured.

Ramsay raised her eyebrows. There was nothing at Ingle apart from the old chapel, Joff Bay, Kenny's house and The Brow. "Oh? Why's that then?"

Fay swung herself into the saddle, which had been extended to its highest point. "I'm going to visit Louie," she said. She rolled forward to test the brakes, which let out a protesting shriek of metal on metal.

"We're not allowed," Ramsay protested.

"*You're* not allowed to see *Daniel*," Fay corrected her. "No one said anything about me seeing Louie. She's my friend. I'm going to visit her."

Thinking back over her dad's words, Ramsay had to concede that Fay was technically right.

"Would you like me to give a message to anyone in particular?" Fay asked innocently.

Having thought of little else all week, Ramsay now went utterly blank. "Just say I said hello," was the best she could do.

20

DANIEL WAS WOKEN from pleasant dreams about Ramsay by the sound of Chet barking in the kitchen. Nobody else seemed to be making any move to investigate so he pulled on yesterday's jeans and a sweater and stumbled down the stairs. He was surprised to see Fay standing at the back door being growled at through the glass by Chet.

"Hello?" he said, once he had unbolted the door and let Chet out into the garden.

"Hello," said Fay, looking curious. "I just called round to see Louie. But if she's not…"

Daniel had already turned away and was at the bottom of the stairs. "Lou. Visitor," he bellowed in a voice that made the whole cottage quake.

"I'm asleep," came back the muffled reply. "Who is it?"

"You'll have to come down and find out," shouted Daniel. "What am I – the receptionist?"

He returned to Fay, rolling his eyes. "She'll be down. Do you want breakfast?" He opened the fridge, which seemed to be full of half-litre bottles of Diet Coke and nothing much else.

"Er, no thanks, I've already eaten," said Fay. She patted her pocket. "I've got some Leaf if I get hungry."

Louie wandered in, smoky-eyed with yesterday's make-up. She was wearing fake-fur slippers and a floor-length towelling dressing gown, which obviously also doubled as an art overall as it was streaked and spattered with paint.

"Hello," she said to Fay in a kind of wonderment at having a visitor. "Did you come to see me?"

"Yes," said Fay. "I thought we could go for a bike ride or something."

"I haven't got a bike," said Louie.

"Why's all this Coke in the fridge?" Daniel demanded.

"Mrs Ivory brought it over for me yesterday," said Louie. "She said you told her I was missing it, so she got someone to bring a crate back from the mainland. Twenty-eight bottles. She said if I can make it last a month she'll get me another crate."

"That was nice of her," said Daniel. "I didn't think she was listening."

"Yeah. She's quite cool. For a teacher," Louie agreed.

"Mrs Ivory is so kind," said Fay. "When James broke his leg playing football and was off school for ages last year she went to visit him every week with food parcels. She's always saying, I want you to be happy. If there's anything that's making you unhappy just come and see me and I'll fix it."

"And does she?" asked Daniel.

"I don't know," Fay admitted. "I've never not been happy."

"I wonder if Kenny's got a bike he could lend me," Louie was saying.

"Is Kenny a friend of yours then?" asked Fay. To the students of Stape High he was just the person you called out if the loos were flooded or there was a dead bird on the tennis courts.

"Not really. He brings us eggs, and vegetables from their garden next door. And he keeps saying I can have one of his kittens, but I can't because of Chet. I used to think he was a retard, but now I think he's just shy."

"He worships Mrs Ivory," said Fay. "He used to go round cleaning windows for free until she gave him a proper job as assistant caretaker, with his own van and everything. Now he practically bows down when she passes him in the corridor."

Daniel picked up a rusty golf club from the broom cupboard, and went outside to practise his swing on rotten windfalls. He trampled down a patch of grass and then lined up a row of apples and began to hit them, one by one, into the trees. The bruised, over-ripe ones exploded on impact.

While Louie disappeared upstairs to get dressed, Fay

wandered out and stood, watching him. "Ramsay said to say hello," she said.

Daniel paused mid-swing and turned, hopefully. "Did she?"

"She's sorry she can't see you. It's not because she doesn't want to."

"I know. She explained. I don't want to get her into trouble."

"Well, she doesn't want to get you into trouble either by breaking her promise to Dad."

"It's OK. Trouble always finds me sooner or later." Another apple disintegrated into a shower of pulp. A thought struck him. "How come you're allowed here, but Ramsay isn't?" he asked.

"Well, Dad never specifically *said* I couldn't. All he said was that Ramsay wasn't allowed to see you. And he doesn't know I'm here, does he?"

Daniel couldn't help smiling. There was something so frank and uncomplicated about Fay that reminded him of Ramsay. As he teed up the next apple, an idea began to take shape in his mind. He brought down the club and caught the apple sweetly, sending it soaring over the trees. When he turned back to Fay his face was glowing. "Will you give your sister a message from me?" he said.

21

WHEN RAMSAY ARRIVED at the stables there was no sign of Joanne, the owner, or any of the other Saturday girls, and the door to the office was closed. Normally at this hour the yard would be ringing with the busy sounds of horses' hooves and voices, and the radio babbling away to itself in the tack room.

Midnight and Bluebell, the colts, and Holly, the chestnut mare, stood gazing solemnly at Ramsay over the tops of their stable doors, but Trampus's stall was empty. Joanne must have taken him out, Ramsay thought, as she let herself into the tack room and put her lunch down on the bench. She noticed that the place was unusually messy, with hats and bridles and open tins of leather polish dumped carelessly. Papers were scattered over the desk along with an overturned coffee cup, and the uneaten remains of someone's lunch. Knowing how particular Joanne was, Ramsay put away the things that had been left on the floor, wiped up the spilt coffee, threw out the abandoned sandwiches, and squared up the papers on the desk, before moving on to muck out Trampus's stable.

She hadn't done more than rake the filthy straw into a pile when she heard the rattle of a car engine and a Land Rover swung into the yard with a white-faced Joanne at the wheel. She returned Ramsay's wave with a look of dismay, and leapt out almost before the car had stopped moving, saying in a stricken voice, "What are you doing? Don't do that!"

"I was just…" Ramsay faltered, as Joanne dashed past her and stood in the empty stable.

"I didn't want anything touched yet," she insisted and then, taking in Ramsay's bewildered expression, added in a softer voice, "You haven't heard?"

"Heard what?" said Ramsay. For once the island's rumour machine had failed her.

"About Trampus." Ramsay felt bad news rushing up to meet her. "Gina took him out yesterday and jumped a ditch. He's cleared it a hundred times before, but for some reason he just clipped the bank and fell badly…"

"But he's going to be all right, isn't he?" Ramsay asked, as though just saying it might make it true.

Joanne shook her head. "He had to be put down. I wasn't even there to say goodbye." Her eyes welled up and she sniffed noisily.

"Oh no!" said Ramsay. "Poor Trampus. What about Gina – is she hurt?"

Joanne shook her head, blinking hard against the tears. "She rolled away, thank God: she's hardly even got a bruise. But she's in a terrible state. She had to leave him in the ditch, all twisted, and run half a mile to the nearest house to call out the vet, and she was there when he… you know. She couldn't get hold of me because I was out on Holly."

"Oh no," said Ramsay helplessly. "I wondered why

it was so quiet here. I tried to tidy up," she added, gesturing towards the tack room.

"Oh, right, thanks," said Joanne vaguely. She was still gazing sorrowfully around the empty stable. "I can't believe he's gone."

Ramsay stood beside her, awkwardly aware that she wasn't providing much in the way of comforting words. But how was she supposed to console someone who was practically old enough to be her mum? She'd known Joanne for years, but they'd never been on hugging terms and she couldn't very well start now. What should she say? When her nan had died of cancer everyone said, *she was ready to go, she'd suffered enough, she's at peace now*, but that obviously didn't apply to Trampus. Another thought struck her: if there was no Trampus, who was she going to ride? Lizzie always took Bluebell, and that left Midnight and Holly for Gina and Joanne, so there wouldn't really be enough ponies to go around. Before she could stop herself the thought materialised into words. "Do you think you'll get another pony to replace him?"

Joanne looked at her strangely. "What? I can't think about that now. I haven't really taken in that he's not coming back."

"No, I suppose not."

Joanne took a last look at the stable and withdrew, closing the door. Ramsay followed her, at a distance, to the tack room, where she found Joanne slumped in a chair, wearing Trampus's old blanket like a shawl.

Ramsay hesitated in the doorway. It seemed a shame just to go home again, having come all this way; she'd been looking forward to her ride all week. And with Lizzie not here, now might be a good time to stake a claim to Bluebell.

"Um, Joanne, is it OK if I take Bluebell out instead then?" she said.

Joanne seemed to have difficulty processing this simple question. "Not really, no," she said at last, looking at Ramsay with a troubled expression. "I think it's best if you go home. I'd rather be alone here today."

"Right, OK," said Ramsay, horribly aware that she

had said the wrong thing. "I'm sorry about Trampus. I wish it hadn't happened." She picked up her riding hat, still containing her lunch, from the shelf by the door and backed out. As she crossed the yard, she heard a stifled sob come from the tack room. Ramsay quickened her pace. As soon as she reached the lane, she began to unpack her sandwiches, calmly eating as she walked along and carefully stashing the litter back inside her hat.

She had just taken a large bite of her apple when she remembered with a jolt that this was the one that she had brought for Trampus and which he would never now need.

What's wrong with me? she thought wildly, almost choking on her apple, and swallowing it in one piece so that it went down like a razor blade. *Why can't I cry like Joanne?* She stood in the middle of the muddy lane and closed her eyes, trying desperately to feel something, other than mild frustration that her day had not turned out as planned.

A long time ago, when she was six or seven, she'd found a mole in the garden, injured, perhaps by a squirrel or a fox. She had put him in a shoebox of straw and tried to feed him milk dripped from a piece of linen. She had sat for hours watching over him, in a daze of love for his tiny pointed snout and pink-gloved paws. They had kept the box in the kitchen by the range to keep it warm, but in the morning he was stiff and cold. She had cried an ocean of tears over his little shoebox coffin, and given him a proper burial under the cherry tree.

She thought of Trampus, her loyal companion over years of Saturdays, imagining his dreamy dark eyes with their thick eyelashes, and the soft velvety kiss as his lips took a sugar lump from her palm, and the way he stood, so still and obedient, while she combed the knots out of his mane. *Trampus is dead*, she told herself, willing herself to feel it. *You will never see him or stroke him or ride him again ever.* She opened her eyes. Nothing.

"What's wrong with me?" she shouted up at the sky,

causing a cloud of startled magpies to rise, flapping reproachfully, from the high branches of a tree, and then she threw the unfinished apple into the hedgerow and began to run.

22

WHEN DANIEL HAD had enough of golf practice and turned to go indoors he saw his mum at her bedroom window, tapping on the glass and beckoning him urgently.

He found her pulling clothes out of her chest of drawers and chucking them unfolded into a small overnight case which stood open on her bed.

"You won't believe it," she said, picking up a pair of dusty leather pumps from the bottom of the wardrobe and giving them a wipe on the bedspread before dropping them into the case. "I've just had a call from our tenants in London. The house has been burgled."

Daniel felt a stab of alarm. He remembered Helen saying that she was convinced someone had broken into

Wren Cottage, and began to imagine a vast and sinister network of spies. If they could find and silence the hospice worker, surely they could reach London. *Get a grip*, he told himself sternly. *It's just coincidence. Someone in our street gets burgled about every five minutes. This time it's our turn.*

His mum, oblivious to his inner confusion, continued her haphazard packing, as she elaborated. "They've lost lots of their own valuables like cameras and laptops and jewellery but they aren't sure how much of our stuff is missing, so I've got to go back and make a list for the insurance company. What a nightmare."

"Are you going right now?" He felt a twinge of resentment at being abandoned.

Into the suitcase went a hairbrush, thickly matted with hair, and a hooded towelling bathrobe. Once white and fluffy, it was now greyish and balding.

"If I get the midday boat and drive non-stop I can get back to London by tonight. Then I can do the insurance stuff tomorrow, visit my editor on Monday morning, drive down to Plymouth in the evening and then get the early boat back Tuesday. Do you mind staying here and looking after yourselves?"

Daniel shook his head. "It's what we do anyway," he pointed out.

For a second his mum looked hurt, but she didn't deny it. "You can come if you want to," she said. "But I can't see Louie volunteering to get on that ferry again in a hurry."

"No way," said Daniel, remembering. She had puked most of the way and the sea hadn't even been rough. He couldn't think of anything worse than being cooped up for hours with Louie moaning and Chet barking and slobbering. Twice.

"You won't mind being here on your own, will you?" his mum asked, crushing the lid down on the suitcase and tugging at the zip. "It's so safe."

If there had ever been a good time to confide in her now was most definitely not it, Daniel decided. In fact, as soon as Mum had gone he would phone Helen and tell her to leave him out of her investigations. He didn't want to get involved in anything remotely dodgy right now.

"Course not."

"I'd better go and say goodbye to Louie and then I'll make a move. There's money in the envelope on the kitchen dresser if you need it for food and things. Make sure you eat that chicken tonight because it's nearly off."

Daniel smiled non-committally. As far as he was concerned those drumsticks were going straight in the bin the minute she was out of the door. Just because his mum was a fanatical sell-by-date denier he didn't see why he should play Russian roulette at every meal. He watched out of the window as she leaned over the fence and called Louie in from Kenny's garden. He predicted, correctly, that she wouldn't want to say anything about the burglary or going away in front of Fay. But Fay made her excuses and left anyway, pedalling off on her rasping clanking bike.

"Don't mention to anyone that I've gone," Mum

insisted, as she hugged them goodbye in the privacy of the kitchen. "I don't want people to know you're on your own. Although no doubt the news will be out before I'm halfway to Port Julian."

"It's OK," said Louie, who was looking a bit unsettled by her mum's hasty departure. She hadn't quite had time to weigh up the advantages of two days in London against the disadvantages of the crossing.

"Can you bring back some pizzas?" she asked.

"I'm not going on a shopping spree," Mum said, doubtfully.

"Oh, and some eye make-up remover pads and nail glue and some Super-hold Root Booster Spray," Louie added.

But Mum was already out of the front door and trundling her overnight bag towards the car. At the gate she turned. "Look after each other while I'm away. You'll be able to get me on my mobile once I'm back on the mainland."

Daniel and Louie watched the car bounce away down

the pot-holed track until the rattle of the engine was swallowed up by the sound of the wind lashing the trees. They looked at each other, smiles bright with a confidence that neither of them really felt. Then they went back into the empty house, closed the door and locked it.

23

DANIEL PICKED UP the phone and, stretching the cable almost to snapping point so that he could withdraw into the dining room and close the door, he dialled Helen's number. Louie was installed in front of the TV watching a repeat of *Dr Who*, and safely out of earshot. Even so, he wouldn't get involved in a long conversation, he told himself. Just a quick hello, sorry I can't help you and goodbye. Half a minute, max. If she wasn't there, so much the better – he could just leave a message with the boyfriend.

But this time it was Helen herself who answered. "Daniel? What's going on? Why haven't you phoned?" she asked before he could launch into his prepared speech.

"Er, I didn't know I was supposed to," he replied, trying to remember if he'd led her to believe he might.

"Well, I can't very well ring you – your mum or sister might answer. Never mind. Are you OK to talk?"

"Yes. I was really ringing to say—"

"Can anyone hear us?"

"No. Louie's watching TV and Mum's probably halfway to London by now."

"She's gone to London?"

"Only for a couple of days – she'll be back on Tuesday."

"That might be useful. Her not being there, I mean."

"Yes, but, Helen—"

"I've been doing some research into Narveng and unless I've completely got the wrong end of the stick, there's something pretty disturbing going on at Stape. I need someone to—"

"Don't tell me any more," Daniel burst out, at last finding the necessary determination to interrupt her.

There was a shocked silence on the end of the line.

"Listen. I'm really sorry, but I don't want to get involved in this."

"But you're already involved," Helen protested. "You're as involved as me now."

"But I never asked to be. The whole point of us coming here was to get away from problems, not go looking for them. It'll kill Mum if I get into any more trouble. That's if she doesn't kill me first."

"There won't be any trouble if you're careful. I just need a… researcher. You're in the perfect position to go into school without anyone asking questions. I wouldn't ask if there was anyone else that I can trust. But there isn't."

Daniel felt himself weakening, and then hated himself for it. *I'm not going to be made to feel guilty about things that aren't my fault,* he thought irritably. People would talk and talk and tie you up in knots with their talking if you let them. Teachers and solicitors and social workers and his own mum – they could bury you alive in words. "But apart from that," he said firmly, saving his best argument for last, "I don't even think there is anything dodgy going on at the school. I've been in there, I've seen what it's like and I know some of the students – they're all totally happy."

"Exactly," said Helen. "They're all perfectly happy all the time. Five hundred teenagers and none of them are ever depressed or moody or stroppy or sad or rebellious. And do you know why?"

"Well…" Daniel began, but a tiny seed of uneasiness had entered his mind.

"Because they're being *drugged*, that's why," Helen burst out. "Every single student at Stape High is being used in a huge experiment, without their knowledge or consent. And we're the only people who can stop it."

24

D ANIEL ARRIVED AT the old chapel at three o'clock, as arranged. The bicycle stood propped against the remains of the wall which enclosed the tiny stone ruin, so he knew she was already inside. He wondered if she'd watched his approach. His heart was drumming hard from the uphill climb that he had taken at a run, and from a mixture of excitement and nervousness at the idea of meeting her again.

The heavy wooden door shuddered and scraped against the flagstones as he pushed it open, releasing a dry, churchy smell of wood and stone and the breath of dead candles. The windows were broken and boarded up, but what was left of the daylight leaked through a hole in the roof, and in the semi-gloom, he could see

Ramsay sitting in one of the pews, facing the bare altar, her back to him. She started slightly at the sound.

"Is that you?" she said.

"It's me," Daniel replied. "Are you all right?"

"I am now you're here. I thought you might not come."

He walked up the aisle and sat in the pew directly behind her, so that he could see the back of her neck and the blonde wisps above her coat collar which had failed to make it into her two neat plaits. "If I say I'm going to do something I do it. I'd never just not turn up."

His message, faithfully delivered by Fay, had said: *Meet me at the old chapel at 3 o'clock on Sunday if you can. No need to reply. If you don't turn up I'll understand. But I'll be there hoping.*

And now Ramsay was here, sitting just centimetres away from him. She'd cycled halfway across the island to meet him, and was doing everything she could to stop his shameful secret becoming local gossip. She was so lovely it made him nervous just to be in the same room with her.

Above their heads, cobwebs thick with dust hung like grey rags. "Keep talking," she urged. "This place kind of freaks me out."

"I'm not going anywhere," said Daniel, and he leant forward and slid his arms around her shoulders. She didn't shrug him off or move away, but reached up and caught hold of his hands in hers and held them.

They sat like that for some time without speaking. At last, Ramsay said, "What have you been doing since I last saw you?"

"Since you slammed the door in my face, you mean? Oh, nothing much. Just plotting and scheming how I could see you again."

Ramsay laughed. "I don't believe you," she said.

"It's true. OK, I took some time off for meal breaks. What about you?"

Ramsay told him about Trampus's accident, and how useless she'd been at comforting Joanne. "I couldn't seem to *feel* anything," she said. "Joanne was blubbing as if her heart was breaking, and I just stood there as if I wasn't the least bit sad. And the thing is, I *wasn't*. Does that make me sound terrible?"

"You were probably in shock," said Daniel, but all the same her words sent a little chill through him. They echoed so exactly what Helen had been saying only the day before.

"That's what I thought. It'll hit me later. But it didn't. I went home and I was fine. And this morning I woke up feeling cheerful, like I always do, and then I remembered about Trampus. And I still felt cheerful. I must be a monster."

Daniel didn't know what to say, so he just wrapped his arms more tightly around her and rested his chin gently on her shoulder.

"And it was the same with you. When my dad said I couldn't see you any more. My mind was telling me: this is awful – I should be crying my eyes out. But I couldn't."

"Oh, you don't want to go crying over me," said Daniel lightly.

"But I never cry about anything. Even when bad things happen. I felt sorry when my nan died of cancer. But I didn't cry at the funeral or anything. My mum and dad did. But I didn't."

"What about sad films?" said Daniel, remembering Louie blubbering over the end of *Titanic*. Of course he hadn't shed a tear over Leonardo DiCaprio himself; the boat couldn't go down soon enough for him. "Or what about *Romeo and Juliet* -- or *Brokeback Mountain*? Louie says that's the saddest film ever. Mind you, she cries at *Wallace and Gromit*."

Ramsay laughed. "They're just stories. You can't feel sad about a made-up story. Can you?" she added.

"Sometimes. But don't get all worried about it," said Daniel, although he felt slightly worried himself.

"I just wonder if I'm missing out on something," said Ramsay.

There was a beating of wings above them as a pigeon

flew through the hole in the roof and perched on one of the rafters, showering them with bits of nest.

Daniel brushed the strands of straw from Ramsay's hair. "Can't have you going home looking like you've been rolling in a haystack," he said.

"What are you going to do when you leave here?"

For a moment Daniel thought she meant later that evening, but then he realised she was talking about when he left the island for good.

"I don't know. Sixth form, I guess. If anywhere'll take me with my record." He stopped, regretting this reference to his past and hoping Ramsay wouldn't follow it up. There were certain things he could never tell, and if she began to question him he would almost certainly have to lie. He couldn't bear the thought of lying to her. "Maybe university after that," he added quickly. "What about you? Do you think you'd ever move away?"

"But where to?"

"I don't know – London. America. Anywhere?"

Ramsay shook her head, as though he had suggested

travelling to some remote planet. "I used to think it would be nice to get away from the island, but I don't suppose I ever will. Nobody does, really. When I was little I dreamed of going to Austria to see the mountains. But not so much lately. Maybe I've grown out of it."

"Don't you ever get that feeling of wanting to escape?"

"Why should I? I'm happy here."

"Because... oh, I don't know," said Daniel, abandoning this line of argument. At the back of his mind he was thinking of something else Helen had said as evidence for her theory. *They're too docile. They've got no ambition. You ask even the really clever ones what they want to do when they leave school and they say: I'll stay here and work at the farm, or the supermarket or the freezing works. Nobody wants to venture out into the big wide world. It's not natural.* All right, Helen, he thought. I believe you. And if Ramsay is being drugged then I'll find the proof, even if I have to take the school apart a brick at a time.

"What we really need," Ramsay went on eagerly, "is

a few more people like you coming over here to live, so we've got some new faces around the place."

Daniel shifted on his seat. The pews had not been designed for this sort of contact and he had to lean forward at an awkward angle, but he didn't want to let go of her.

"This is the weirdest date ever," said Ramsay, and began to laugh. "If anyone walked in right now…"

"It would be kind of hard to explain," Daniel agreed. He looked around, at the thick coating of dust on the pews, and the cobwebs and the bird droppings spattered on the altar. "But it doesn't look as though anyone has set foot in here for about ten years, so I think we'll probably be OK."

He leant in to kiss her neck, but when he was just millimetres away his watch beeped the hour, very close to Ramsay's ear, and she leapt. He sprang back, glad that she hadn't seen him fumble this basic manoeuvre.

"Is that four o'clock already?" she wailed. "I've got to go. I said I'd be back at five. And that bike is so useless. It'd be quicker to walk." She stood up "You go first," she said. "Make sure no one's around. I'll wait for a minute to give you time to get out of sight and then I'll go."

"OK." He stopped by the door. "Ramsay. Can we meet again tomorrow?"

"I've got basketball after school… but I could come out later – like seven-thirty?"

"It'll be dark. You won't be scared of this place in the dark?"

"Not if you're here."

"I'll be here," he promised.

25

As RAMSAY NEARED home, a stiff breeze was blowing from the direction of Stape, carrying with it the faint smell of bonfires. This wasn't unusual for the time of year and besides, her head was full of Daniel, so she didn't give it any thought. But the next day the whole village was buzzing with news of a serious fire at the school.

It had started in the groundsman's hut – a wooden shed on the back of the sports pavilion, which contained ladders, paint, petrol-mowers, tools and other maintenance equipment. After the retirement of the previous groundsman, his duties had been taken over by Kenny, who was at home tending his chickens. So the only witness was the caretaker, whose cottage was some distance away, near the main school block. At three o'clock he had heard the crash as the windows blew in, and come out of his front door to see the pavilion engulfed in flames. He'd also noticed a figure -- no more than a blurred shape – running away through the woods on the margin of the playing field.

On Monday the students and staff had all been kept behind after assembly and a police officer from Port Julian asked anyone with information to speak to him afterwards in the strictest confidence. But nobody apart from the caretaker had anything to report. There was a general sense of outrage about the loss of the pavilion, which was a relatively new facility – built at the same time as the swimming pool and paid for by the same anonymous benefactor. Mrs Ivory was credited with securing this funding, and she expressed her great disappointment to the assembled school, but reassured them that the pavilion would be restored to its former glory. Outside forces, she said, echoing her speech at the 4th of October fireworks, would not be allowed to undermine their wonderful school.

Ramsay relayed all these details to her parents that evening as the family sat around the kitchen table eating a rather stringy lamb casserole.

"Very peculiar," said Mrs Arkin, chewing grimly. "You hear of these pupils who get expelled and then come back and try to burn down the school. Not here, of course. I mean in America." She gave a little grimace of distaste, which may have been aimed at a particularly tough piece of lamb or at the general idea of America itself.

"No one could have a grudge against our school," Ramsay was saying. "No one's ever been expelled."

"No one's even been in detention since I've been there," Fay added.

"I was looking through the court archives today," Mr Arkin said. "There hasn't been a case of arson on Wragge since 1857."

Ramsay's heart gave a gallop. She knew where this was going.

"I'm wondering," he added, "if I ought to tip off the

police about our friend at The Brow." His tone of voice was anything but friendly.

"It does seem to be a bit of a coincidence," his wife agreed.

Ramsay and Fay looked at each other in alarm. "Daniel wouldn't do a thing like that!" Ramsay protested.

"But the fact is, he already has done," Mr Arkin pointed out.

"Well, that still doesn't mean he did it this time," Ramsay insisted, swallowing hard. A lump of gristly lamb sat like a stone, halfway down her gullet. She knew beyond any doubt that Daniel wasn't involved. At the exact time the fire had broken out he had been on the other side of the island in the ruined chapel with her. But this was the one alibi he couldn't use.

"You said you wouldn't tell," she said quietly.

"These are exceptional circumstances," her father replied. "Anyway it would just be a quiet word in the inspector's ear."

"There's no such thing as a quiet word around here,"

Ramsay said. She knew how it would be. At the first breath of gossip against them, Mrs Milman would pack up and move the whole family back to London. Daniel had more or less said as much. And then she would never see him again.

She laid down her knife and fork across her plate of almost untouched lamb. "Thank you for the lovely dinner," she said. "Please may I leave the table?"

"Of course," said her mum, oblivious to any change in atmosphere.

Concealing her extreme urgency to get away, Ramsay scraped her unwanted food into the bin, stacked her plate and cutlery in the dishwasher, and strolled out of the kitchen. It was only when she was safely out of the house and on the rickety bicycle that she allowed herself to hurry along the dark and empty lanes towards the ruined chapel.

26

THE IT SUITE was more crowded than it had been on Daniel's previous visit, and he had to angle his monitor slightly to ensure that his nearest neighbour couldn't see the screen. This precaution was hardly necessary, as his neighbour – a serious-looking boy of about twelve – was fully occupied in designing a complicated piece of circuitry. But Daniel was taking no chances.

At the end of their telephone call on Saturday, Helen had promised to email him some of her research about Narveng and it was this that he was now reading, with a racing heart and one eye on his watch. He had two hours until his meeting with Ramsay, and he wanted to make sure he was early so that she wouldn't have to spend any time alone in the chapel. Even he had to admit it would be creepy after dark.

Hi Friend (Helen was obsessive about not using his real name).

Here's a summary. If you still don't want to get involved, I can't force you, but please regard everything that follows as STRICTLY CONFIDENTIAL and delete it when you've read it. If you want to do any more research don't use the school computers – go to the library in Port Julian.

Narveng is a pharmaceutical company which makes prescription and over-the-counter drugs. Their biggest sellers are medication for asthma and hay fever, but they make literally hundreds of other products. For the last five years they've been working on a drug called Compound K for treating depression. You may or may not know, but existing anti-depressants have a whole range of unpleasant side effects – including anxiety, paranoia and depression! Useful, eh? The potential market for an anti-depressant without side effects is vast – we're talking billions – given that about one in five people are, or think they are, depressed.

Compound K is at an early stage of development — it's been tested on primates and a small sample of human volunteers — but needs a long-term and large-scale trial before it can be licensed for sale to the public. Within a couple of days, those first volunteers reported complete relief from symptoms of depression. Even those with a history of violent mood swings became placid and contented—

There was a rustling noise close beside Daniel and he looked up sharply. His neighbour had produced a paper bag from his pocket and was slowly transferring the contents, one leaf at a time, to his mouth. With a sense of slowly dawning realisation that made his scalp prickle, Daniel looked around at the rest of the students working silently at their computers. Without exception, they were chewing the same frothing cuds of green pulp, their faces wearing matching expressions of dreamy contentment.

All was quiet apart from the distant hum of a floor polisher, and the gloop and gurgle of the water coolers, as Daniel roamed the empty corridors of the school. He had no clear idea of what he was searching for or where he should look for it. His mind was still buzzing from the revelations in Helen's email, and the shock of finally accepting that she'd been right all along. He was convinced that Leaf was the key to the whole conspiracy, but he still couldn't understand why the students would willingly eat something so revolting. Even if it was one of those sophisticated flavours that grow on you over time, the first taste would put anyone off for life.

Helen's last line had been: *If you do want to help, you need to find material evidence that links Compound K and Narveng to the school.*

It was hard enough to find something you had lost in a space no bigger than a house when you knew exactly what it looked like. How could he begin to search the whole school when he didn't even know what he was looking for?

He'd left the classrooms behind and was now in a part of the school he had no excuse to be in – the admin block, consisting mainly of teachers' offices and storerooms. At the far end of the corridor, someone had left their keys hanging from a lock. The key ring caught Daniel's eye because he had an identical one in his pocket – an orange rubber fish which doubled as a torch. When you squeezed its gills a light shone out of its mouth.

He hesitated in front of the nearest unmarked door, wondering how he would explain his presence if he was discovered. He pushed it open, ready to retreat if necessary, but it contained nothing more exciting than a photocopier and reams of different coloured paper, ink cartridges and bottles of toner.

On a sudden whim he lifted the lid of the photocopier and found that the last item to be copied had been left face down on the glass. His hopes were immediately dashed as he turned it over and found it was nothing more than a letter to parents about the cancellation of the Christmas concert, owing to the sudden departure of the music teacher.

Daniel almost laughed at himself for feeling so unreasonably disappointed. As if anyone would have conveniently left some incriminating document just lying around! What had he expected – a letter from the chief executive of Narveng marked 'Top Secret'? Asking how the 'experiment' was going?

He decided to abandon this hopeless searching and set off for the chapel to wait for Ramsay. But as he walked back towards the main foyer something was niggling at him. At the very edge of his consciousness was the merest blur of an idea which refused to come into focus. If he turned the full beam of his attention on it, it would vanish altogether, so instead he tried to distract himself by counting down from a thousand in blocks of thirteen like he used to in Lissmore.

He had reached 857, and was just passing through the unmanned reception area to the exit, when it came to him. He stopped abruptly, leaving the automatic sliding doors twitching uncertainly back and forth.

Keys in a keyhole. In a place where nobody ever locks anything.

Daniel spun on his heel and headed back the way he had come, into the admin block and past the offices to the last door on the left, from which the key ring still dangled. Now what? He knocked gently, ready to leg it if anyone replied, and then again more forcefully. There was no answer. He let himself in to what turned out to be another storeroom, and pulled the door to, just as he'd found it. Along one wall was a row of large cardboard boxes, stacked two high and three deep. There were no markings visible to give any indication of the contents; only a row of arrows showing which way up they should be stored. None of the boxes was sealed so Daniel opened the flaps and checked the contents. Again, disappointment: each one contained a twenty-litre refill for the water coolers – nothing else. Beyond the boxes in the corner were stacks of paper drinking cones wrapped in polythene, and on the opposite wall were shelves bending under the weight of giant loo rolls and liquid soap dispensers, paper towels, cleaning fluid, disposable gloves, light-bulbs of every shape and size, catering packs of instant coffee, teabags and plastic spoons, but nothing remotely relevant to Daniel's search. He was just about to leave when he heard the sound of footsteps approaching along the corridor. Instinctively he drew back into the narrow gap between the boxes and the wall, crushing himself up against the paper drinking cones, waiting for the steps to pass. His chest tightened with alarm as the footsteps grew louder and louder and then halted. Then he stopped breathing altogether as the door briefly swung open before it was pulled shut again and the key turned in the lock.

27

I T WAS DARK when Ramsay reached the ruined chapel a few minutes after seven-thirty, and she desperately hoped that Daniel would already be there. She unclipped the headlamp from the front of her bike and, in the sweep of its bright conical beam, could see that the heavy oak door was slightly ajar.

"Hello? Daniel?" she called through the gap in an amplified whisper, which seemed to echo in the stony silence. No answer. Disappointed and more than a little anxious, she let herself in and stood inside the door, shining the lamp around the interior of the chapel, across the tops of the pews and into the dusty cobwebbed vaults of the roof. Slowly, mastering her nervousness, Ramsay walked down the aisle, wishing she had thought to bring another torch or some candles. When she reached the front pew where she and Daniel had sat together, she stopped. Even though he wasn't here now it looked as though he had been earlier, because half a dozen leather prayer cushions had been arranged on the hard wooden bench to make a comfortable couch. He'd evidently thought of candles too, as there were splashes of dried wax on the floor. But where was he?

Ramsay sat down on the padded seat and waited, playing the torchlight around the walls and hoping the batteries would last. Next time she would definitely bring candles. As she concentrated on listening out for Daniel's approach, she became aware that the silence wasn't really silence at all, but a whole symphony of creaks and sighs and rustles. She could almost hear the dust particles colliding.

Ten minutes passed, then fifteen. Ramsay was glad of her thick winter coat and scarf, because the hole in the chapel roof meant that it was hardly warmer inside than out. *He'll be here any minute*, she kept telling herself, with less conviction as the time went on. *I'd never just not turn up*, he had said last time and she had believed him. But what could be keeping him? His journey from home was far shorter than hers: ten minutes' walk at most. How long should she wait before giving up? Ten more minutes, she decided, wishing she had some means of leaving him a note. It was then that she heard the crunch of feet on the path and a moment later the scrape of the heavy wooden door catching on the flagstones. Her heart bounded with relief and happiness.

"Hello," she called eagerly, and when there was no immediate reply from the shadowy doorway added less confidently, "Daniel? Is that you?"

28

I T TOOK DANIEL a few seconds to realise that he was
locked in. As he hesitated between his first instinct
to hurl himself at the door, and his second to remain
concealed, the footsteps moved off briskly down the
corridor. It was too late. A sense of self-preservation
stopped him from calling out, as well as something like
fear – fear of having to explain himself, of the trouble
he would be in, of having failed at the very first hurdle
and letting Helen down.

But as he eased himself out from the tight space
between the boxes and the wall and the now flattened
paper cones, he felt another kind: the fear of being
imprisoned. It was the first time he'd been in a locked
room since he left Lissmore. He had to close his eyes

and take deep slow breaths to beat back a rising tide of panic.

Keep calm, he told himself. *It's just a room. Nothing bad can happen.* As his pulse rate returned to normal he opened his eyes and tried to work out what to do next. He thought of all the adventure stories he'd read – a locked door never proved any kind of barrier if you had a paper clip or a bent hair-pin. If only I'd got locked in the stationery cupboard, he thought.

More out of superstition than hope, he tried the door, just in case it wasn't really locked. Then he tried his house keys, jiggling and tweaking them in the lock, with no success. Frantically he searched the shelves for something that might stand in for a paperclip. But there was nothing suitable amongst the supplies, and he wasted valuable minutes and several disposable spoons before conceding that plastic was no match for a sturdy metal lock. So he turned to the only other escape route – a small louvre window. Its six slats of toughened glass were four inches wide and opened to an angle of forty-five degrees. Daniel could just fit his arm up as far as the elbow through the gap between each of the slats. Even if he had a club hammer as a weapon he doubted the glass would break. *At least I won't suffocate*, he consoled himself, breathing in the damp autumn air. Although he could only see sky and the tops of trees through the slanted glass, he worked out that it gave on to the corner of the field by the cricket nets. Outside, dusk was falling, and it was only now that Daniel made another unwelcome discovery. There was no artificial light in the storeroom and soon it would be completely dark. Since coming to Wragge, Daniel had become used to the absolute blackness of the nights without streetlamps or traffic, or the background glow of the city – but it would certainly not make trying to escape any easier. Soon the only sources of light he had were his fish key ring, producing a bright but pencil-thin beam, and the backlit face of his watch, which gave out about as much energy as a decaying corpse.

He glanced at the time, picked out against the bluish

glow, and remembered Ramsay with a jolt that made his heart kick furiously against his ribs. It was seven-thirty. She would be waiting for him, alone and anxious in the dark ruined chapel, wondering where he was, or worse, thinking he'd changed his mind – after all his promises only the day before. He felt a volcanic pressure of rage and frustration boiling up inside him and before he could stop himself he swung a punch at the wall. It took the skin off his knuckles and made his whole arm sing with pain. He slid to the ground, clutching his ruined hand while the darkness deepened around him.

29

THE DRAUGHT FROM the open door stirred the cobwebs above the altar. "I was about to give up and go home," Ramsay called out, wondering why Daniel didn't reply. She'd expected apologies and excuses at the very least, and had already imagined her own generous reply. There came back the silence of held breath, and for the first time it dawned on Ramsay: *it's not Daniel.* Before she could react, the heavy door banged and she heard footsteps running, slithering away down the path.

Ramsay jumped to her feet in fright, fumbling the bicycle lamp, which fell to the ground and promptly went out, stranding her in darkness. Whimpering with fear, she groped in the dust under the pew until she found it and, praying that it wasn't broken, located the switch with shaking hands. The glass had cracked in half but the bulb still worked. Ramsay wildly raked the walls with its beam, to check that there was nothing lurking in the shadows before she fled down the aisle and out of the door. Her bicycle was lying in the long grass where she'd left it. She pulled it up and ran with it, jamming the lamp back on to its bracket without breaking her stride. And then she was up in the saddle and pedalling like crazy. The headlamp illuminated no further than ten metres ahead, but every so often a waxy moon came bowling out from behind the clouds and she could see the fields and hedges flying past her. Where the path forked, she chose the turning for The Brow, slowing slightly as the gradient began to bite. There was Winnie and Kenny's house ahead, sheets blowing palely on the washing line, the bluish light of the TV flickering in the window, and the sight of these ordinary things gave her courage.

It occurred to her that whoever it was who had stood there in the chapel entrance without speaking, had heard her calling Daniel's name, and now knew that she'd been expecting him. She wondered who it could have been, and why they had run off without saying hello, since they must have recognised her. She couldn't think of any reason why someone would have come to such a remote spot, which was not on the way to anywhere, and had been derelict for years.

As she neared the top of the hill, The Brow loomed into view, like an ocean-going liner, every window lit up. From over the garden wall came the sound of barking, and a figure moved in the shadows. It was Louie, letting Chet out for a last run around.

"Louie," Ramsay called, bringing the bike to a skittering halt by the gate. "It's me."

Shading her eyes from the glare of the headlamp, Louie approached, calling to Chet, who had his front paws up on the wall, ready to vault over it if provoked.

"Oh, hi, Ramsay," she said, clipping the dog's lead back on, and tugging him away. "Have you seen Daniel? I thought he was with you."

"No. That's why I came. He was supposed to meet me but he didn't turn up. I got a bit worried," she added. "I mean, he wouldn't just not show up, would he?"

Louie shook her head. "He sometimes forgets to do things," she admitted. "But only things he doesn't want to do in the first place."

"I just thought… well, I hope nothing's happened." Since the fireworks Ramsay had been slightly tentative about encountering Louie again, remembering her freak-out, but she seemed perfectly placid and easy-going tonight.

"Come in a minute," said Louie, keeping a tight hold of Chet as she opened the gate. "It's cold out here. Mum's in London," she added as Ramsay followed her towards the house. "So I'm all on my own."

"I didn't know that," said Ramsay. In her view this made it even more unlikely that Daniel would deliberately leave Louie alone with no idea where he was.

Inside, the kitchen was in a state of chaos. The sink and draining board were piled high with unwashed plates and pans. The bin was full to overflowing, and there was a pile of empty Diet Coke bottles and other rubbish beside it. On the table was a stack of unopened post, the remains of Louie's dinner, a jam jar of paintbrushes soaking in some murky green water, a pair of trainers and an apple with a bite out of it.

There were muddy paw prints on the floor, things crunching ominously underfoot, and a grubby streak around the walls and cupboards at dog height. Ramsay tried hard not to look taken aback at the mess, for which Louie offered no apology or explanation.

"Daniel left about four," Louie was saying, brushing crumbs from two of the chairs so they could sit down. "He said he was going over to the school and then seeing you. I thought he meant he was meeting you there."

"No, no. We arranged to meet at the old chapel. Because, you know, it's out of the way. But the weird thing is, someone did come into the chapel while I was there. At first I thought it was Daniel, but they ran off before I could get a look at them."

"Did you hear a car or anything?"

"No, they were on foot."

"But who was it?" Louie asked. "There's only us and Winnie-next-door for miles around."

"You don't think it was Kenny, do you?" asked Ramsay. "I can't really see Winnie making it up that hill without collapsing."

"It wasn't Kenny," said Louie. "I've just been round there to see the kittens and he was mending his van."

"Well, whoever it was, it still doesn't solve the problem of Daniel. Do you think he's all right?"

"I don't know," said Louie helplessly. "He goes off without saying when he'll be back, even at night sometimes. But if he said he'd be somewhere, he would be."

"Do you think we should call the police?"

"No," said Louie, horrified. "Daniel would kill me if I called the police."

"Well, someone else then."

"I don't know anyone else. We haven't got any friends

here. We've never even had a visitor – apart from Mrs Ivory."

"You could phone her. She'd know what to do."

Louie's expression was doubtful. "Look, I'm sure he's OK. He can look after himself better than anyone I know."

Ramsay glanced at her watch. "I'll have to go home soon or my parents will start asking questions," she said in a worried voice. "But I don't want to go without knowing that he's all right."

"I could walk with you as far as Stape," Louie suggested, "if you ride slowly. Maybe we'll meet him on the way. Or I could ask in the village if anybody's seen him. At least we'll be doing something. I'll bring Chet," she added, glancing at the dog, lying prone under the kitchen table.

Ramsay agreed eagerly so Louie put on a fleece, and scribbled a note to Daniel, in case he somehow missed them on his way back and got home before her. *Daniel, where the hell are you,* she wrote and then frowned and crossed it out. If he was reading the note then he was in the kitchen! She settled on *Daniel, me and Ramsay have gone to Stape to see if we can find you. We've got Chet. Lou xx* and left it on the kitchen table propped against the trainers. The two girls set off in the direction of Stape, one riding slowly, the other walking briskly, with Chet trotting along between them.

30

B Y THE LIGHT of his fish torch Daniel was examining
the louvre window. Each of the glass slats was held
along its two short edges in the rigid PVC casing of the
frame, and opened parallel with one another. Daniel
reckoned he would only need to remove three slats to
create a space big enough to squeeze through – but the
fit was so tight they refused to move. Still, driven by the
thought of Ramsay waiting for him in the old chapel,
and Louie, worrying at home all alone, Daniel was
determined to exploit the room's only weak point. Using
one of the broken disposable spoons, he forced a sharp
splinter of plastic between the PVC and the glass, on
each side, working it up and down, pushing against the
long edge of the pane until he felt the glass shift forward

a fraction. The movement was microscopic – no more than a millimetre – but it made Daniel's heart lurch with renewed hope. There was a chance he might escape without giving himself away. He didn't care how long it took – what were a few hours compared to four months in Lissmore? If it was just a question of time and effort and patience: he would do it.

He bitterly regretted punching the wall earlier, because his stronger right hand was now painful and weak – and this was a job that required two steady hands. The darkness didn't help. As he needed both hands, he was forced to hold his torch clamped in his mouth, squeezing the gills together with his front teeth to keep it alight. Being unable to close his mouth reminded him of being at the dentist. Every few minutes he kept gagging on his own saliva and had to drop the torch to stop himself choking.

It took an hour and a half to remove the first pane, leaving a gap between the sill and the next pane of about fifteen centimetres. He laid it on top of a cardboard box closest to the window, and set to work on the second. This time he was quicker; perhaps his technique was improving or the glass was just a looser fit, but within an hour the second pane was lying on top of the first. He tested the space – he could stick his head right out, and if he'd had an accomplice strong enough to lift him and post him through the slot like a parcel, he might not have needed to remove the third pane.

A faint sound from somewhere outside in the blackness made him withdraw hastily. Distant voices, barely audible, came floating towards him from across the expanse of field. If this had happened two hours earlier he might have been tempted to call out for help, but he wasn't about to give himself away now so he shrank back and waited for the sound to die out.

When he was sure there was no one within earshot, he began work on the third pane. He was reluctant to use the fish torch in case the tiny point of light was visible to whoever had been passing, so he worked in the dark by touch alone, easing the shards of plastic spoon under the PVC, wincing with pain as he slipped and jabbed his hand. After fifteen minutes he reinstated the torch, but it still took a further hour of painstaking probing, scraping, pushing, and easing before the job was done. It was just before midnight when he stood in front of his escape hatch.

Using one of the large cardboard cartons to give himself a leg up, Daniel carefully wriggled through the gap until he was lying across the sill on his stomach. He shifted around on to his back, clutching at the remaining slats for support, and pulled himself up into a sitting position, with his legs dangling into the room. Then he gradually shuffled back, lowering himself towards the ground until he could work one leg free. The drop from window to ground level was further outside than in, and he ended up falling the last metre or so in an ungainly heap on to the gritty tarmac. Winded and grazed, but triumphant, he clambered to his feet. He felt invincible: no walls could hold him.

Now he was faced with a dilemma. Louie was at

home by herself and might be worried – frantic even. He should get back as soon as possible to reassure her. On the other hand, Ramsay had been stood up, abandoned in that creepy old chapel in the dark, and he was desperate to see her and explain. He was torn. *Louie or Ramsay? Ramsay or Louie?* Who had first claim? Ramsay's house was only minutes from school – he practically had to pass the end of her lane to get home – whereas Louie knew about his night wanderings, so might actually be fast asleep. Plus, she had Chet, he persuaded himself, so she wasn't really alone. Hadn't he done enough for her over the years?

Daniel batted these arguments back and forth as he jogged towards the sleeping village, imagining that he hadn't yet made up his mind. But when he came to the turning for the path back across the moors to The Brow he ignored it, and carried on towards Ramsay's house.

Outside the café on the green where he had first spoken to Ramsay, nearly three months ago, was an old-fashioned red telephone box. He'd never noticed it before, but now it seemed like the answer to his dilemma. He would call Louie and reassure her that he was OK. Then he could go and see Ramsay with a clear conscience.

Daniel still didn't know the number for The Brow, but inside the phone box was a copy of the Wragge telephone directory – neither stolen nor defaced: another small miracle of island life.

He went to look up Milman, then remembered the listing would still be in the name of Ericsson, his great-grandfather. There it was between Easterhouse, Dr A.J. and Evergreen the Florist. He dialled and listened impatiently as the phone rang on and on unanswered. "Come on, Louie, pick it up," he muttered into the mouthpiece, frustrated by this new delay. He could picture her upstairs in bed, sleeping peacefully, oblivious and deaf to any interruptions. But as he hung up and walked away from the phone box, he felt slightly uneasy. *I tried*, he told himself, quickening his pace as he reached the end of Ramsay's road. *I did try*.

31

THE TWO GIRLS and Chet reached Ramsay's house at half past nine, having walked for more than an hour meeting no one on the way. "Well," said Ramsay, who had expected nothing less, "what now?" She could see her mum moving about the lighted kitchen, opening and closing cupboards, assembling the ingredients for an evening snack.

"You go in," said Louie. "I'll walk as far as the school, and then go home, I guess. If he's not there by the time I get back I'll phone Mum. She'll know what to do."

Reassured by this solution, Ramsay opened the front gate and wheeled her bicycle inside, and then returned to give Louie a goodbye hug. They had become friends on the course of the walk, and she felt that her previous view of Louie as unbalanced and moody was unfair.

"Tell you what this place needs," Louie said as they had exchanged hugs, "mobile phones. I don't know how you manage without them. This whole problem would have been sorted in five minutes flat."

"Some mobile company wanted to set up a mast here a few years ago. There was a big meeting about it in Port Julian. Loads of people were against it, saying mobiles were like little microwave ovens and we'd all get our brains fried. So when it came to a vote nearly everyone voted no. I've never really felt like I needed one. Until now."

The two girls parted and Louie set off towards the village, keeping Chet on a short lead. She was beginning to regret her generous offer to walk with Ramsay now that she was alone and so far from home. If it wasn't for Chet beside her she'd have felt nervous walking in the countryside at night. Although she felt a bit anxious about Daniel she knew he'd be all right, because he was the strong one in the family, the one they all leant on. Even in Lissmore when they'd gone to visit him, she and Mum had been the ones in tears – he'd had to reassure them. *I'm fine. Everyone's really friendly. The time's going so quickly.*

The village was deserted, and there were only a few lights on in the houses opposite the green. Even if she had been the sort of person to approach a complete stranger to ask if they had seen Daniel, there was no one to ask. Apart from a curtained glow from the caretaker's cottage, the school buildings were in darkness. The burned-out pavilion was only visible as a blackened shape. She wished she could remember why Daniel had been going to the school, but she wasn't sure he'd told her. She made a slow circuit of the playing field to put off the inevitable moment of going home to make the promised phone call to Mum. Just as she reached her starting point, she heard the sound of a car engine approaching on the Filey road. A moment later headlights swept past her, drenching her in their brightness. The car pulled up some way ahead and began to reverse slowly until it drew alongside, and Louie recognised Mrs Ivory at the wheel. Relief washed over her. Not a stranger, but someone who had been kind to her on two occasions and would know what to do.

The window slid down. "Hello, Louie," said Mrs Ivory, leaning across the passenger seat. "I thought it was you. You're a long way from home. Is everything OK?"

"Daniel's missing," Louie said. "I don't know where he is." Just saying it seemed to lift a huge pressure from her shoulders, as though the problem of his absence was a heavy weight, which Ramsay had passed to her, and she was now handing on to someone else.

"Oh," said Mrs Ivory, with a sympathetic frown of concern. "Well, you can't go looking for him on foot. Jump in and we'll drive around and see if we can find him." She swung the passenger door open.

Louie looked doubtfully from Chet to the clean leather interior. "My dog's a bit dirty. He normally sits on a hairy old blanket."

"Oh, you don't need to worry about the car. People are more important than things. People and dogs, I mean."

As Louie climbed in the back with Chet, she noticed a key ring swinging from the ignition, and the familiarity of it made her smile. It was an orange rubber fish – just like Daniel's.

32

RAMSAY LAY IN the darkness, wondering what had woken her. Tired after her journey across the island, she had fallen asleep quickly, but now she was awake again. It was after midnight. Everything was quiet apart from the comforting creaks of the house settling itself for the night. Being awake while others slept gave her a feeling of loneliness she never felt at any other time. She turned over in bed, trying not to disturb the tunnel of warmth she had created, and then she heard it: a pattering, scrabbling sound, like a small animal scurrying over the wall. It wasn't loud, but it was near – just outside the window. She sat up in bed and tweaked the curtain open. As she peered over her pots of Leaf into the darkness, a handful of loose earth hit the glass directly in front of her face and slithered down on to the sill. She opened the window as another handful caught the edge of the frame, showering her with soil.

"Ramsay," hissed a familiar voice from the shadows of the garden. "It's me." Her heart leapt.

"Daniel," she whispered back. "Stop throwing dirt at me. Where were you?"

"Can I come in for a minute?"

"Well…" Ramsay was doubtful.

"I just want to talk to you."

"The front door creaks really loudly. We'll get caught."

"I'll climb up."

Before she could reply he'd already started to clamber up the elderly Russian vine which smothered the side wall of the house. Its trunk was as thick as his arm, solid and twisted like rope, and there was a network of newer thinner branches clinging to the stonework. *Romeo*, she thought, with a combination of admiration and fear at his recklessness. But it didn't seem to be nearly as easy for Daniel as it had been for Romeo, and for a moment Ramsay worried that he was going to pull the whole thing off the wall and end up on his back in the flowerbed. Hastily shifting several pots of Leaf out of the way, she grasped his arm and helped to drag him inside. With the curtains closed the room was so dark that she couldn't see him. They sat opposite each other on the bed, knees just touching.

"Ramsay," said Daniel, reaching blindly for her hands and grasping them in his.

"Daniel, this is insane."

There were two closed doors and a length of landing between them and Ramsay's parents, but they spoke in whispers nevertheless.

"I know, but I really wanted to see you."

"You're freezing," said Ramsay, shivering at his icy touch. The night air seemed to stream from his clothes. "We could get under the covers," she said shyly, twitching back the duvet and shuffling over to make room for him.

He scuffed his trainers off, and then slid in next to her. They lay side by side, their heads very close on the pillow, hardly breathing.

"You smell nice," he said at last. "Like shampoo and clean clothes."

He rolled over to face her, and she could feel the roughness of denim, zips and buckles pressing through the soft jersey of her pyjamas. "I'm sorry I wasn't at the chapel. Did you wait long?"

"Twenty minutes or so."

"I would have been there, but I got locked in a cupboard at school."

"What?"

"Someone locked me in a storeroom. By accident -- I don't think they knew I was there."

"There aren't any locked rooms at school."

"There is one. I've just spent about three hours breaking out of it. I kept thinking of you sitting in that creepy old chapel by yourself... I was so frustrated not being able to get to you."

"I knew there had to be a good reason. I'm just glad you're OK. How did you get out, anyway?"

Daniel described his painstaking escape from the room. "So all I've done tonight is climb in and out of windows," he finished.

"Anyone would think you were a criminal," she murmured, and then it came back to her – what she'd needed to tell him so urgently at the chapel. "You know about the fire at school?"

"No. What fire?"

"Someone set fire to the pavilion. It's completely burned out. The police came up to the school and everything."

"Oh my God," said Daniel.

"I know. You were in the chapel with me when the fire broke out. But nobody else knows that."

Daniel exhaled heavily.

"I wondered whether the police had come to ask you about it. Because if they had it means Dad must have told them about you."

"No one's said anything to me about it. Don't worry – I won't give you away."

"But you must," Ramsay insisted. "If you're accused of something you didn't do, I'll say you were with me."

"You're so nice," said Daniel, then paused. "Ramsay," he said, in a new and serious tone, which made a blush sweep over her. "If I asked you to do something for me, would you do it, without asking why?"

"Well… OK."

"Will you give up eating Leaf? For me."

The request was a little disappointing. Ramsay had expected something more personal. "All right, if it means so much to you," she said, feeling slightly trapped by her pledge.

Daniel found her hand and squeezed it. "Thank you," he said. "If there's anything you want me to do in return, just say."

Ramsay thought for a moment. "No. There's nothing about you I'd want to change." The darkness made her brave enough to pay him this huge compliment.

For a moment they lay in silence, thinking separate yet remarkably similar thoughts. "I wish I could stay here all night," he said at last.

"I wish we could meet all the time like normal people," said Ramsay.

"That would be nice too."

"The chapel's off limits now," Ramsay added. "Someone else is using it." She explained about the mysterious visitor, the rearranged prayer cushions and the spilt candle wax, playing down her hasty exit. Safe in bed, with Daniel beside her, she wondered how she could ever have been afraid.

"It can't have been Kenny, because Louie said—" She stopped abruptly. *Louie!* She hadn't given her another thought. "Have you seen Louie? Does she know you're OK?"

"I tried to call her from the phone box but there was no reply. She must be asleep. She could sleep through a rocket attack."

"She was worried about you. She went looking for

you around the village. After waiting in the chapel I called at your house and we walked back here together. If she couldn't find you she was going to phone your mum."

Daniel groaned quietly. "Oh no." He sat up, and began hunting for his trainers beside the bed. "I've got to go." She heard him dragging them on, and felt the bed quake as he clambered across her to open the window. Chilly night air flooded into the room.

"Be careful. Goodbye," she whispered. As she knelt up he leant back and pulled her towards him and kissed her hard on the mouth, stifling her gasp of surprise. His arms were round her, clasping her against him, and she was kissing him back. *Nothing will ever be better than this moment*, she thought. James had never kissed her like this. Just as it began to seem that Daniel had abandoned any plan to leave, he broke away.

"I'll think about you all night," he promised, and then he was out of the window and scrambling down the vine. She heard the thud as he dropped the last couple of metres into the flower bed. She lay back on her pillow, her face burning, wondering how long it would be until they were together again.

33

"DOES DANIEL OFTEN go wandering off like this?" Mrs Ivory asked, as the car cruised the dark and deserted streets of Stape before heading out on the road to Filey.

"Sometimes," Louie admitted. "But if he goes out at night he usually takes Chet."

"Perhaps he's called in on a friend?"

"I don't think he's got any friends. Except Ramsay and Fay, but he's not with them. I suppose there might be someone else he hasn't told me about," she added. Daniel had no trouble keeping secrets.

It took twenty minutes to perform a circuit that took in the settlements of Filey and Darrow and brought them back to Stape, without passing Daniel or anyone else on the way. "The thing is," Louie said, as the school came into view again, "he might have arrived home while we've been driving around, and we wouldn't know. Perhaps I'd better go back."

Mrs Ivory had taken a left turning past the terraced row where Helen Swift had lived, and instead of following up Louie's suggestion, swung the car down a narrow tree-lined road. After a while it gave way to an unmade track terminating in an open gate. "How about we go back to my house and you can phone from there?" Mrs Ivory said. Since they were now pulling up outside the front door Louie could hardly object.

Although it was dark, Louie could see that the house was similar in size and shape to The Brow, but in a much better state of repair. Mrs Ivory let her in to a bright and welcoming hallway, with freshly painted walls and a polished wooden floor, free of the dust, dog-hairs, discarded shoes and general clutter that Louie associated with home.

"The phone's in here," said Mrs Ivory, showing Louie

into the sitting room. A coal fire had nearly burned out in the grate; Mrs Ivory stirred the embers with an iron poker and threw a shovelful of coals on top, then withdrew to the kitchen to make coffee, followed by Chet.

Louie dialled home, allowing herself a flutter of hope that Daniel might pick up. She hung on long after it was clear that he wouldn't, until she was finally cut off. She replaced the receiver and looked about her, noting to her dismay Chet's dirty paw prints on a cream rug – the only blemish in an otherwise spotless room. Apart from an alcove of bookshelves, there was little to suggest anything about the owner. The only furniture was a pair of red sofas facing each other across a low coffee table. On the white walls were various colourful and splodgy paintings, which might or might not have been Art – Louie wasn't sure.

Above the fireplace was a huge black and white framed photo of a girl of about fifteen, staring out of a window looking thoughtful. She had long dark hair and an intelligent face and bore a strong resemblance to Mrs Ivory, who came in at that moment carrying a tray.

"Any luck?" she asked, unloading steaming coffee and a plate of thick white toast, running with butter.

"No," said Louie, who had stationed herself on top of Chet's paw prints. "I'll try again in a minute."

"You stay here in the warm and eat that lot up, and I'll go out again in the direction of Port Julian. I'll be back in about twenty minutes."

From the kitchen came the sound of Chet drinking noisily. "I gave him a bowl of water," Mrs Ivory explained.

"You can shut him in there if you don't want him rampaging around the house," Louie suggested, helping herself to coffee. She was cold and thirsty, and gulped it down too quickly, gasping as it tore at her throat.

"He's all right." Mrs Ivory gave the fire another prod with the poker. "I'd like a dog myself, for company, but it doesn't seem fair if I'm out at work all day." She straightened up and, noticing that the portrait over the mantelpiece was tilted fractionally, readjusted it.

Louie said, "That's a nice picture. Is it you?"

"Oh no," said Mrs Ivory, though she seemed pleased with the comparison. "It's my daughter, Hilly."

"I didn't know you had a daughter. Have you got any other children?"

"No. Just Hilly. Unless you count the five hundred students at Stape High, of course."

"She's so pretty," said Louie, who was always ready to acknowledge good looks in others.

"Yes, she was," said Mrs Ivory. "She never thought she was, even though I kept telling her." She paused, then continued, "I'd better be heading off. Make yourself comfortable and keep phoning home. I won't be long."

Louie heard the front door close with a soft click. She felt herself enveloped in the silence of an unfamiliar house. She ate the toast and finished the last gritty dregs of coffee, and then rang The Brow twice, hanging on each time until she was cut off. The coal fire was giving out some heat now, and she allowed herself to doze drowsily on one of the red sofas until a scampering noise made her sit up. Venturing out into the hall, she found the rest of the house was in darkness. Louie couldn't understand this mania of grown-ups for switching off lights. *They may as well still live in caves*, she thought, patting the wall in a vain search for a switch. In the gloom Chet appeared at the top of the stairs. He had something in his mouth; long pale ribbons trailed from his jaws.

"What have you got there?" said Louie, bounding up the stairs and catching hold of him on the landing. She gently prised the item from his teeth. It turned out to be a satin ballet shoe, now horribly chewed and soaked with slobber.

"Chet, you bad dog. Where did you get this from?" Louie demanded. With supreme indifference Chet sat down and began to lick himself.

All the upstairs doors were closed apart from one which was ajar, allowing a weak and flickering light to leak on to the landing. Still holding the mangled shoe, Louie let herself in and looked around, unable to stifle a squeak of surprise and alarm. A single chubby candle stood burning on the windowsill. Its sputtering flame reflected in the blackness of the glass behind it, throwing distorted shadows on to the walls, and in the darkest corner of the room stood the ghostly figure of a girl, all in white. "Oh!" Louie gasped. The figure didn't move.

Quaking with fear, Louie scrabbled for the switch and snapped on the light. Only then did she realise that the girl was just a dressmaker's dummy modelling a long gauzy ballet dress. Even so, it was a few minutes before Louie's heart-rate returned to normal. She was in a bedroom, evidently belonging to Hilly, since there were cuddly toys on the bed and dozens more photographs of her on the walls, along with framed certificates for dance, music and gymnastics. A glass-fronted cabinet contained various amateurish pieces of pottery and needlework – the sort of stuff Louie would bring proudly home from school for Mum, who would demote it rapidly from mantelpiece to back of wardrobe to bin. In front of this was a music stand holding a piece of sheet music, covered in pencilled instructions – *Dynamics! Count! C#!* A violin lay in an open case on the desk as though practice had been interrupted and might resume again at any moment.

Louie located the partner of the ballet shoe at the end of a rack of neatly arranged sandals, trainers and ice skates, wondered if she could possibly get away with replacing it without explanation, then decided she couldn't. This Hilly character was fanatically tidy and would totally notice even the slightest disturbance to her things. As Louie looked around, it struck her that, even making allowances for over-tidiness, there was something about the room that wasn't quite right. No normal girl, surely, would choose to cover her walls with pictures of herself? Louie's bedroom at The Brow was decorated with posters of bands, a family portrait from before The Divorce, a blurry photo of her guinea pig who had died, and a selection of postcards from a trip to Tate Modern.

Here it was all just Hilly. You'd have to have massive confidence in your own appearance to enjoy being surrounded by so many images, but hadn't Mrs Ivory said Hilly never thought she was pretty?

Then Louie suddenly understood. The pictures, the belongings, the candle burning in the window, all made sense. She backed out swiftly, silently, and closed the door, with the solemnity and respect that is owed by the living to the dead.

34

DANIEL WAS AWARE of a diffuse orange glow in the
sky over in the direction of The Brow, long before
the house itself came into view. Although he was tired
and cold again after the warmth of Ramsay's bed, and
hadn't eaten since lunchtime over twelve hours ago, he
was still buzzing with excitement from that kiss. He could
hardly believe he'd dared to grab her like that, half
expecting her to tense up and push him off, but she'd
kissed him back. He'd thought his head would explode,
and it had taken every atom of self-control to get back
out of that window...

Striding on through the night, he felt strong enough
to overturn a car, uproot a tree with his bare hands, or
take on a pack of wild dogs. But there were no wild

dogs to be faced, just a solitary fox, whose eyes blazed yellow in the torchlight, before it slunk through the hedge and away over the fields.

He was surprised to see every light on in The Brow, as though a party was in full swing, and still more unsettled when he opened the front door and there was no Chet bounding up to greet him.

"Hello?" he called, with a sinking heart, moving through the empty rooms. "Louie?"

He stood helplessly in the kitchen. It was some minutes before he noticed the message Louie had left for him amongst the clutter. It wasn't particularly enlightening, telling him nothing more than he already knew from Ramsay and giving no hint of where Louie had headed. She'd been gone more than five hours! The fact that Chet was with her was only mildly reassuring. Where the hell could they be?

Just as he was contemplating the almost unbearable idea of heading out once again into the cold night to look for them, the phone burst into life, its sudden shrilling in the silent kitchen making him leap. He snatched it up, fumbling it to his ear in his haste. "Hello?" he said with a trace of desperation in his voice.

"Oh," said Louie. "You're there."

"Louie! Where the hell are you? I was getting really worried."

"Looking for you! You're the one who's missing – not me," she reminded him.

"Yeah, sorry," said Daniel, trying to master his frustration, "I just got back and there's no one here so I got a bit… you know. Have you got Chet?"

"Yes, he's with me. I've been ringing home every twenty minutes. What have you been doing?"

"It's complicated. I'll tell you later. Where are you ringing from, anyway?"

"I'm at Mrs Ivory's house."

"*What?*"

"I bumped into her when I was out looking for you. We drove around a bit trying to find you, then she brought me back here so I could keep phoning, while she went out in the car searching again."

"Oh *God.*"

"It's OK, she's totally cool about it. She's just coming in the door now. I'll tell her you're OK."

"Have you spoken to Mum?"

"Not yet."

Daniel blew out a long sigh of relief.

Through the muffling of the receiver he could hear Louie saying, "Daniel's back; he's on the phone," and then something he couldn't catch, and the next voice was Mrs Ivory's.

"Daniel – you're safely home," she said calmly. "That's wonderful. Louie was getting just *a little* concerned."

"Yeah. Sorry. I got a bit held up, and then I called in on… a friend… and I forgot the time… and—"

"As long as you're all right," she said, cutting off this stream of inadequate excuses.

"Yeah. I'm fine. Sorry you've gone to a load of trouble."

"It was no trouble. Now, since we've established everyone's all right, and it's rather late, Louie may as well sleep here in my spare room, and then I'll drop her back first thing in the morning."

Daniel would have preferred it if Louie and Chet had come home, but having caused so much disruption, he felt he could hardly start making demands. And he was so grateful that Louie was OK, and that everything had been sorted out without involving their mum, that he would have agreed to anything.

As soon as he had hung up, relief gave way to extreme hunger. He took an over-ripe banana from the fruit bowl of wizened apples and ate it in three bites. The kitchen was in a state: it would need a major clean-up before Mum got back, but not now. Daniel realised he was missing her. Even though it might not seem that she did much when she was here, everything fell into disarray when she wasn't. Maybe she did stuff without him noticing.

He wandered around switching lights off and then

wearily climbed the stairs. Even removing his trainers required a monumental effort, and he toppled into bed without bothering to undress, and fell asleep where he landed.

35

DANIEL WAS WOKEN just after eight the next morning by the sound of Louie, singing along to the radio in a bright clear voice. He found her in the kitchen, attempting to clear a space on the table amongst the clutter. There was a warm, toasty smell coming from the oven. Chet, who had been circling around the table, sniffing for spilt food, came bounding over, jumping up and almost pushing Daniel over in his enthusiasm.

"Get off me, you crazy hound," Daniel laughed.

Louie turned at the commotion. "Hello," she said cheerfully.

"I never heard you come in," he said.

"I didn't want to wake you up," said Louie. "You looked so peaceful." She opened the oven and a gust of hot bread-scented air filled the room. Bringing out two crusty rolls with bare fingers, and dropping them hastily on to a plate, she said, "Mrs Ivory stopped at the baker's on the way back in case we didn't have anything in the house."

"That was nice of her. Sorry you had to stay over. I tried ringing as soon as I could, but…"

"That's OK. I had quite an interesting time." She split the rolls with her fingers and spread them thickly with butter before offering the plate to Daniel. He hesitated for only a second before choosing the largest, promising himself that he'd be unselfish some other time when he wasn't so starving.

"Oh yeah?" he asked, through a mouthful of bread.

"No. You first. Where were you last night?"

Daniel gave her a detailed account of the hours he had spent in the locked storeroom, and an edited account of his night visit to Ramsay. Louie kept interrupting with questions and expressions of disbelief. "Why didn't you just smash the window?"

"Because it was reinforced glass and there wasn't a handy brick lying around."

"Those voices you heard – that must have been me and Mrs Ivory. You should have yelled out."

"I didn't need to by then. I knew I could get out by myself."

"Ramsay wanted to call the police. She really likes you."

"I know she does." He hadn't mentioned the kiss, but the memory was never far from his mind. He only had to close his eyes to relive every detail.

"Why were you snooping round the storeroom in the first place?"

"Because I wanted to know what was so important that it had to be locked away in a place where nothing is ever locked away."

"You could just ask Mrs Ivory. They were her keys."

"*What?*"

"You said it was a fish key ring like yours. It belongs to her. I saw it in her car ignition last night."

Daniel was shocked into silence. He had assumed the caretaker or a cleaner had locked him in. "How many keys were on it?" he said at last.

Louie put her head on one side, as she always did when trying to remember something. "Two, I think. One in the ignition and one dangling. Why does it matter?"

"Because if that's her only key apart from her car key it must be important. There must be some reason for keeping that room locked – even though there's nothing valuable in there. Other rooms with computers and musical instruments and expensive equipment are left wide open."

"Why are you so bothered?"

Daniel opened his mouth and then shut it again. He couldn't think of a way to explain which wouldn't involve explaining everything. "I can't tell you… yet," he said. To his surprise, Louie made no attempt to follow this up. Usually she would have pounced on a remark like that and demanded to be told, then nagged and moaned and cross-examined him until he gave in. But she just shrugged placidly. "So, anyway," he went on, not quite believing he'd got away with it, "tell me about Mrs Ivory's house. What's it like?"

"Nice," said Louie. "Pretty. It's got bare wooden floors and white walls, with red sofas and a cream rug and…"

Daniel swallowed the last of his bread, lost in thought. He was sure Mrs Ivory had to be involved – it was her keys that had locked him in, and he was now sure it had been her who had disposed of the drawstring bags with the Narveng logo on them. She had been there on the footpath from the beach the day he had found the bag in the bin. And she had seen him with it just before he used the school pool. "But is it flash?" Daniel interrupted. "Is she rich?" He wanted to know whether her house suggested the sort of lifestyle that a teaching salary couldn't buy. After all, whoever was providing Narveng with access to hundreds of human guinea pigs would surely have to be generously paid. Daniel couldn't imagine any other possible motive for taking such a huge risk.

"Not really. It's no bigger than this. It's *cleaner*, but it's not flash. She hasn't even got a TV."

So if not money, what was in it for her? He realised Louie was still talking away, and that he hadn't been paying attention.

"I said I thought I might start school after Christmas," Louie repeated.

"What? Why?"

"I thought it might be fun. It's getting kind of boring at home. And Mrs Ivory said I'd be in Fay's class."

Daniel stared at her, horrified at this turnaround. Knowing what he now knew, Stape High was the one place in the world he'd never let her go. His protestations were cut short by the ringing of the telephone. He snatched it up.

"Hi, Mum," he said, recognising the sharp sucking-in of breath before she had even said a word.

"Oh, someone's there at last," she exclaimed. "I rang four times yesterday until midnight."

"Ah," said Daniel. "We were out."

"I sort of gathered that."

"I was at Ramsay's," he improvised, "and Louie was at a... er... sleepover. How did you get on, anyway? Was anything stolen?"

"Only a couple of paintings – nothing valuable. Oh, and my identity."

"What? Where are you?"

"I'm stuck at Port Julian. This place gets madder by the minute. They won't let me through because 'according to their records' I'm already here. Apparently someone calling herself Ingrid Milman landed at Darrow airport on Sunday."

36

D ANIEL AND LOUIE stared at each other across the kitchen table. "Why would anyone pretend to be Mum?" he wondered out loud.

"Even Mum doesn't want to be Mum," said Louie. This struck Daniel as the truest thing Louie had ever said, and he burst out laughing, until she couldn't help joining in.

But the fact was their mum was stuck at Port Julian until someone in authority could confirm her identity. "People here have no sense of urgency," she had complained, before ringing off. "I could be here all day."

"The problem is, nobody knows what Mum looks like," Daniel grumbled. "She's such a hermit."

"Mrs Ivory knows. She'd help, I know she would.

And the people at customs would respect anything she said."

"School's started by now," said Daniel. "She can't go waltzing off to Port Julian halfway through the morning."

"She can do anything she wants – she's in charge!"

"You ring her then."

Daniel left her to it and went into the garden with Chet, who was pawing at the back door and whining to be let out.

The chilly morning air felt heavy with damp and the trees were draped with mist. The dog whisked around the garden, his nose to the grass following scent trails, and returned to Daniel with the remains of an old tennis ball in his mouth. The green felt had been gnawed into loose flaps and now resembled a small cabbage. Daniel obligingly lobbed it high in the air and watched Chet caper back and forth excitedly until it landed with the flabbiest of bounces and he could seize it again.

As the repetitive rhythms of the game cleared Daniel's head smothered half-thoughts began to surface. Louie was so different lately – so easy-going. He'd been so obsessed with Ramsay that he'd hardly noticed at first, but soon after the fireworks she'd seemed to calm down. In fact for the last week or so she'd been really docile.

Docile. That wasn't his word. Someone else had used it, recently, but not about Louie. He threw the ball almost vertically and watched it shudder, flap and come to land in a patch of Leaf that was growing in the long grass. As he went to put his foot over the ball – a manoeuvre which drove Chet into a frenzy – he noticed that someone had dug a clump out of the middle – a socket of fresh soil was clearly visible.

Instinctively he glanced back at the blank face of the house. Louie's curtains were open and between them on the windowsill stood a small terracotta plant pot, from which tufts of green foliage sprouted. Abandoning Chet's game, he strode towards the house, his heart thudding.

Louie was standing at the open fridge with her back to him. In one hand she held a bin bag into which she was dropping various items of out-of-date food. "It's all sorted," she said, without turning round. "Mrs Ivory was in a meeting, but she took the call. I knew she would. She said as soon as it's over – in about twenty minutes – she'll drive down to Port Julian and—"

"Louie," Daniel interrupted her.

She spun round, surprised at the urgency of his tone. "What?" she said, revealing teeth stained a livid green.

"Why are you eating Leaf?" he demanded. "You hate it."

"I used to. But it's actually really nice."

"Oh my God," said Daniel wildly. "Spit it out. Spit it out." He grabbed her by the shoulders and she cringed away. "Do you want to end up like all the rest of them?"

He tried to poke his finger between her teeth and scoop out the leaf pulp before she swallowed it.

"Stop it," Louie begged him, frightened, half gagging. "What are you doing, Daniel?"

"You mustn't eat it – it's a drug. Everyone at school is on it, that's why they're so weird and… and… happy. Spit it out."

"But I like being happy," said Louie. "I've been eating it for at least a week and it hasn't done me any harm."

"But it might do. You don't know if it's safe. You're just being used. They're using you all." Daniel was striding about the kitchen, swearing and banging his fist on the table.

"Who is?"

"Mrs Ivory and Narveng," he ranted.

"Daniel. You need to calm down," said Louie gently.

He stopped abruptly and looked at her. Louie telling *him* to calm down. It was such a reversal of the natural order that for a second he was speechless. The sound of a car engine made them both glance out of the window. An elderly police car, the pale blue of a washed-out sky, was bumping up the lane towards The Brow.

"What do *they* want?" said Louie.

"Me," Daniel groaned, watching as the car pulled up at the gate, and a single uniformed policeman got out. "Ramsay said they'd be after me about the fire."

"But the fire was nothing to do with you. Why should you worry?" Louie said.

He gave her such a look that she blushed.

"Just say you don't know where I am," Daniel instructed her, and before she could even reply, he'd slipped out the back door and run across the grass, between the apple trees and away through the gap in the brambles.

He looked at his watch. Mrs Ivory would be leaving the school in twenty minutes and the round trip to Port Julian would take at least another forty. That would give him just enough time. He followed the footpath in the direction of Joff Bay and then cut back along the edge of a freshly ploughed field, keeping close to the high hedge. At the stile, from which there was a clear view of the lane as it curved past Winnie's house, he crouched down and waited until he saw the police car pass back the way it had come. Then he jumped over the stile and ran, tripping and stumbling over the furrowed earth, past fields of stubble, and up on to the moor. He kept to the trails that he knew from walks with Chet, well away from the solitary tarmac road which bisected the plateau, taking the most direct route to Stape. At a steady run, he made it to the school in forty minutes and arrived sweating and breathless, his lungs on fire, just as the bell was ringing for end of break. Pupils were streaming back into the building. He hung back in the shadow of the caretaker's cottage until everyone was inside, and then skirted around to the staff car park. Mrs Ivory's black Ford Focus was missing, her designated parking space empty. Good.

Catching sight of himself in the shiny surface of a parked car, he mopped his sweaty face with his sleeve, and raked his fingers through his hair so that he didn't look quite so wild, before entering the school through the back door to the admin block. He walked briskly, with a confidence that he didn't really feel, as though he was on an important errand.

He stopped outside Mrs Ivory's office and knocked at the door, his heart drumming, prepared to take off at the sound of her voice. But there was no noise, apart from the distant trill of the telephone in reception. He let himself into the room and closed the door behind him. She had evidently left for Port Julian in a hurry – a coffee mug was on the desk, half full and still slightly warm. And, as he'd hoped, she had left her computer on, midway through some work, without logging off.

On this occasion he was going to take every precaution. He slipped the catch up on the window so that it appeared to be closed, but could be pushed open from either side, and then looked around for somewhere to hide. The only possible place was a slim metal wardrobe with sliding doors. It contained a navy overcoat, an academic gown, a reflective tabard, a pair of shoes and several reams of printer paper. Once these had been pushed to one end, there was just enough room for Daniel to squeeze inside.

Satisfied, he sat at the desk and began to work. Mrs Ivory had abandoned the computer halfway through checking emails. With clumsy shaking hands, Daniel typed the word Narveng into the search field. Nothing. He tried

Compound K, but again drew a blank. Disappointed, he tried the recycle bin. Here were deleted files going back *eight years*. He shook his head over this: Mrs Ivory obviously thought just pressing delete actually deleted something.

This time he was lucky. Performing a search for Narveng brought up an email, six years old, from someone called d.chancellor@narveng.co.uk. He could feel his pulse racing with excitement as he waited for it to open. Like all computers on Wragge it was unbearably, prehistorically slow; you could practically hear cogs grinding. It was the first thread of evidence that actually linked Narveng to the school and, more specifically, to Mrs Ivory.

Dear Emma

I enjoyed our meeting and found it extremely productive. Your ideas have set me thinking and I'd be very interested in taking things further. Perhaps we could meet in London?

Dave

Nothing exactly incriminating, thought Daniel, but it was a link. The reply was even briefer:

> Dave
> *This is my work email. In future please use the Hotmail address I gave you. Thanks.*
> Emma

This sounded more like someone with something to conceal.

Daniel glanced at his watch. Even if the border officials at Port Julian liked to do things at a leisurely pace, Mrs Ivory was unlikely to tolerate any time-wasting. There was surely only a matter of minutes until she returned.

He returned to the original message from 'Dave' and clicked on Reply. *This will stir things up*, he thought, cracking his knuckles then beginning to type.

Dave

Just to let you know that I'm pulling out of the Compound K experiment as of now. We've got problems with the students.

Emma

He clicked Send. The pressure of his finger on the mouse was like pushing a button to set off an explosion hundreds of miles away. Somewhere, he hoped, at a desk in the offices of Narveng UK, there would be a man called Dave having a panic attack.

Beside him the phone suddenly rang, its tinny jangle slaughtering the silence, and making him jump up in alarm. Before he could decide whether to make a swift exit or hide it stopped. When he looked back at the computer screen there was a message, which he read with a smile of something like triumph spreading across his face.

What???? What do you mean by problems? You can't just pull out! There's only another two months to go. Anyway, they can't just stop taking K – it has to be a phased withdrawal. We discussed all this! We need to talk urgently.

Dave

PS OK to use this email address now?

Oh my God, Daniel thought. *It's true. It's actually true.* And this was the evidence. For a second or two he considered printing it off right now on Mrs Ivory's own printer, but then he had a better idea. He forwarded the email from Dave to his own Hotmail address, and was trawling his memory for Helen Swift's details when he heard footsteps approaching. With fumbling fingers, he deleted the exchange with Dave and cleared the screen, and then scrambled into the metal wardrobe, setting the coat hangers shivering on the rail and making the whole structure quake. He clutched the hangers and pulled the sliding door across so that only a knife-edged gap remained. He could see a tiny stripe of carpet, wall and window. Immediately a feeling of claustrophobia engulfed him.

The office door opened and closed softly and a moment later Daniel heard the pneumatic hiss and creak of someone sitting down on the swivel chair, followed by the scrape and rustle of drawers being opened and searched.

Only now it occurred to Daniel, crouching awkwardly in the restricted space, and scarcely able to breathe, that he hadn't really thought things through. Mrs Ivory might well be comfortably installed for the rest of the day. How long could he remain hidden, when the slightest twitch would give him away? It was one thing to be found in Mrs Ivory's office, but quite another to be caught hiding in a wardrobe. Various appalling scenarios of discovery and humiliation began to play out in his mind. He wondered whether it would be better to burst out and confront her.

The chair hissed and creaked again as its occupant stood up, oblivious to the storm of emotions raging in the metal wardrobe in the corner, and walked across to the filing cabinet under the window. For the briefest second as she crossed the room she was clearly visible through the paper-thin gap in the sliding door.

Helen Swift.

37

DANIEL WAS SO astounded that for a second or two he froze, unable to trust the evidence of his own eyes. But there she was again, quite unmistakably, caught in that tiny visible strip of room, and heading directly towards him as though intending to check out the contents of the wardrobe for herself.

He was about to call out to her when the office door opened again. There was an electric silence – the sort that flows between people recovering from an unpleasant surprise – then Daniel heard Mrs Ivory say, "Helen! What are you doing here?" Her voice was polite, professional and without a trace of warmth.

Daniel shrank back inside the wardrobe, thanking God that he hadn't chosen that moment to emerge.

"I assume you haven't come to ask for your job back. I know that you gave me false references, although I've no idea why. That's quite a serious offence."

"Quite serious," said Helen. "But not as serious as some other things."

"I've no idea what you're talking about. You've committed a criminal offence. I don't know why the police didn't pick you up at the border," said Mrs Ivory. Her tone was still smooth, but she sounded slightly less assured.

"Let's ask them, shall we?" said Helen, moving towards the telephone, out of Daniel's line of vision. "Give them a call."

There was a click of the door closing. "I'm a busy woman. You've got two minutes to tell me why you're here, and then I'm going to have you removed from the premises."

Helen gave a snort. "Who by? Kenny? He's your loyal slave, isn't he? He's the one who searched my cottage, went through my things. I could smell the chlorine."

"What do you want?" Mrs Ivory's voice was cold but unafraid.

"I want to know why you're doing it. I know what you're doing to the kids here, that you've been medicating them for years, you and Narveng, but I just don't get why. What's in it for you? At first I thought it must be money. But you live in an average house, drive an average car, don't own any property. You haven't even had a holiday in eight years."

"What are you – some sort of journalist?" said Mrs Ivory in a tone of deepest disgust. "The thing with journalists is that you're so corrupt you imagine everyone else has the same grubby morals."

"You're very self-righteous for someone who's been deliberately poisoning children."

"That's a lie. Do you think I would risk a hair of these children's heads?"

"There are risks in any drug. Especially one that's untested."

"It wasn't untested. I took it myself for three years. I was one of the first volunteers."

"Why?"

"Because I had nothing to lose. You've never had a child, have you, Helen?" She went on without pausing for a reply, "Well I have. And I lost her. She took her own life at fifteen. I tried everything to keep her, but she wouldn't stay."

"I didn't know that. I'm sorry."

"She'd tried every pill for depression you can name, but they made her paranoid or dopey or fat or sick, so she stopped taking them. If Compound K had been around ten years ago she might still be alive. And if what I've done here saves just one young life, then it will be worth it."

"But you can't go round drugging healthy people without their consent!" Helen protested. "One of them might have had a violent reaction to it. Someone could have died."

"That's why I took it myself first. And I'm still taking it. About six months after Hilly died I read an advert in a science journal asking for volunteers for a drug trial, and I thought: what have I got to lose? If it kills me, so much the better. But it didn't kill me. It saved me."

"And Narveng never paid you a penny for any of this?"

"They paid me for that initial trial – like all the volunteers. I gave it to The Samaritans. I told you, I'm not interested in money. I've got no one in the world to spend it on. I don't even spend the money I earn."

"And then, after that, you decided to test it out on a whole school? Was that your idea or Narveng's?"

"Mine. The school wasn't like it is now. The buildings were crumbling, there was vandalism and graffiti, the children weren't achieving. They were miserable. And there were so many teenagers like Hilly, at the mercy of their emotions. You know how vulnerable teenagers are; tormented by their hormones. Like that new girl at The Brow – what's her name – Louie."

Daniel, who had been listening with a growing sense of amazement, nearly stopped breathing.

"She reminds me so much of my Hilly. She's got scars all the way up her arms from stubbing out cigarettes on her own skin – can you imagine that? But that's what they're like: they can't handle these violent changes of mood. I thought if we can just get them through that brief dangerous time, think of the benefits to themselves, their families, the whole community…"

"But Emma," Helen's voice was incredulous. "Most people navigate those years without any serious problems. You can't medicate them all on the off-chance that you might save a few."

"Why not? You've seen them. They're happy. They love school, they love home. They love the island. They don't want to leave."

"But it's not real happiness. It's a *chemical* happiness," Helen protested. "And you say there are no side effects, but there are. They've got no feelings. They can't appreciate music or art or beauty, because they can't feel the sadness in it."

"You want them to feel sad? That's perverse."

"And they've got no ambition. They're happy to sit around all day smiling and eating that bloody Leaf! You know, at first I thought Leaf *was* the drug, but when I started researching I realised it was just another side effect. Compound K screws up your sense of taste – it makes sweet things taste bitter and bitter things addictively sweet." Daniel gave such a jolt of surprise at this that for an awful moment he thought he had given himself away. But the women's voices flowed on, uninterrupted.

"I admit it takes away your appetite for sugar, but that's surely a good thing. Leaf is actually very nutritious." Daniel could hear the smile in Mrs Ivory's voice. As he listened to these revelations, he kept remembering things that had struck him as bizarre in his early days on the island: dozens of students crawling around the field scavenging for Leaf; the café that sold only coffee and a bitter lemon drink; the woman at the cinema who said they were the first young people to buy ice cream in years. All these details had seemed odd at the time, but he'd never worked out the connection.

"In fact Leaf has turned out to be very useful," Mrs Ivory was saying. "Because all the time the students keep eating Leaf, I know the drug is still working, and they are still taking it."

"Maybe I can accept that you haven't done this for personal gain. But it's still wrong. It's still an assault against every single one of those kids," replied Helen.

"I love the students at this school. You just want a good story – you don't care what happens to them as a result. What we've got on this island is special. It's a perfect society; people are contented and fulfilled and safe. Everyone looks after everyone else. There's no poverty, no crime—"

"There is crime!" Helen said, her voice rising in frustration. "*You're* the criminal!"

Mrs Ivory ignored this interruption. "If you run this

story, and turn the island into a media circus, it will destroy this community. You want to take me down, but if you do, you'll bring everyone else with me. All I'm asking for is two months. By then the trial will have been running for five years and will be complete."

"You must be insane. I'm not inclined to give you two more minutes in charge of this school. And what exactly have you got to bargain with?"

"You're not in a strong position yourself, Helen. You don't have any actual evidence against me. If we called the police out now, it would be you they'd arrest, not me. The most senior police officer on Wragge is a governor of the school. Do you think he's likely to believe the ravings of someone he already knows has used fake references to obtain a job? After your hasty departure, I've got to tell you your reputation took a bit of a bashing around here."

"I'm not interested in involving the police. All I ever wanted to do was uncover the truth."

"We're more alike than you think, Helen. We're both on a kind of crusade."

"There's no comparison."

"Except, of course, you intend to make money by selling your story."

"You may not have been paid yourself," Helen retorted, "but I bet it was Narveng who put up the millions for the swimming pool and the pavilion and all the other new buildings over the last few years."

There was the silence of a remark hitting its target.

"Just two months. And then I'll tell you whatever you need to know about Narveng."

"Aren't you afraid of what they might do to shut you up?"

"Helen, I'm not afraid of anyone or anything. I told you before: the worst thing that can happen to a person has already happened to me. I've nothing left to lose."

Hearing this, Daniel felt his sympathies oddly divided. He was supposed to be on the side of Helen, and exposing the truth, and yet it was hard not to feel sorry for Mrs Ivory too. Helen herself must have felt something similar as when she spoke the hardness had gone from her voice. "There's still one thing I can't work out. How did you get the drug into them, day after day?"

"Come with me," said Mrs Ivory. There was a scrape of metal as she swept her bunch of keys off the table. "I'll show you."

The door swung closed on their receding footsteps and at last Daniel was alone.

He tottered out of the wardrobe, racked by cramp and dazzled by the daylight. He collapsed on to one of the visitors' chairs and massaged his knotted muscles. His head ached and he had a rampant thirst. *Helen's here now; let her deal with it*, he told himself. But in another corner of his mind lurked the uneasy thought that it wasn't over yet.

As if to confirm this, fire alarms began to wail all over the school, ripping into the silence of morning lessons. Within seconds there was a rumble of feet as students began to stream along the corridors, down the stairs and out on to the field.

38

DANIEL WATCHED THE evacuation through the window, as the alarm continued to peal through the empty building. The students were milling about and staring back at the school with a mixture of excitement and panic. Teachers were herding them away from the building towards the ruined pavilion, barking instructions, and marshalling classes into orderly lines so that registers could be taken. The lab technicians and support staff stood in a huddle, shivering without their coats. The deputy head appeared with a megaphone and, through a storm of feedback, began to tell everyone to leave the premises without re-entering the building. There was no sign of Mrs Ivory.

Daniel opened the study door, half expecting to smell

smoke, but there was instead the musty smell of damp. He walked towards reception, wondering whether to make his escape through the car park or try and find Helen. The carpet felt strangely wet and mossy underfoot, and as he reached the lobby he almost slipped on the thin film of water covering the polished floor. He looked up at the ceiling for a leak, but there was nothing dripping from above, and beyond the windows the sky was blue. A distant sound of footsteps made him glance down the corridor leading past the science labs. One of the doors opened and Mrs Ivory emerged. In one hand she was holding a small sharp knife, which she wiped casually on the sleeve of her jacket before disappearing into the next room. Daniel shrank back against the wall to avoid being seen, his mind whirling in confusion and fear.

Mrs Ivory was clearly mad and dangerous and had probably killed Helen while he dithered. Why else would she be stalking the corridors with a knife, and Helen nowhere to be seen?

Daniel stepped out of the shadows, water lapping at

the toes of his shoes, just as Mrs Ivory came out of the furthest lab. If she saw him she gave no sign of it, but hurried on her way, around the corner and up the stairs. A moment later he could hear running feet above him and classroom doors banging.

He followed after her, and peered into the first lab, his heart quailing at what he might find. But instead of Helen, he discovered the source of the flooding. The water cooler in the corner had been slashed. Water pumped rhythmically from a three-inch slit in the clear plastic casing, spreading around the benches and under the door in a thin glassy layer.

It was the same in every classroom, as Daniel tracked Mrs Ivory's hectic progress around the school. All the water coolers had been sabotaged, their contents forming tributaries which merged in the corridors into thin streams and ran down the stairs. The siren had stopped and the building seemed to resound with the aftershock of sudden silence.

Daniel caught up with Mrs Ivory in the pool block,

in the same changing rooms, he now realised, where she must have followed him to retrieve the bag with the Narveng logo he'd found on the beach. She must have been astonished to see him carrying it around school.

She was jabbing the knife into a water cooler as he came in. It made only a small puncture so that the water emerged in a fine jet that arced across the benches and hit the opposite wall. Irritably she plunged the blade in harder, yanking it back and forward. A curtain of water flopped out over her feet. Daniel could see that the hand holding the knife was covered with blood, and for a split-second his courage failed him. But at that moment she looked up and saw him. There were bright spots of colour on her cheeks, as though she had a fever.

"Daniel," she said, distractedly. "You shouldn't be here. Didn't you hear the alarm?"

"Where's Helen?" he said, without taking his eyes off the knife and the bloodstained hand that gripped it. "What have you done with her?"

"Helen? You're not in this with Helen?" She looked

genuinely let down, hurt even. "I knew she must have had help, but you never crossed my mind."

Daniel shook his head. "I didn't want to get involved in any of this." That will be on my gravestone, he thought. "We came here to get away from trouble, but I always seem to find it."

"Well, I won't pretend I'm not disappointed," said Mrs Ivory, sounding for a moment as though she was an ordinary headteacher and he an ordinary pupil, in her office for a ticking off.

"Where's Helen?" he said again.

"Oh, look what I've done," Mrs Ivory said, ignoring the question as she examined the deep clean cut across her palm. "The plastic on these canisters is lethal. Only one more." She strode out of the changing room towards the pool and up the stairs to the viewing gallery, her high heels echoing on the tiled floor in the vast cavernous room. The last water cooler was in the corner of the gallery. She slit it open and rinsed her injured hand in the outwash.

Daniel, unnerved by her bizarre behaviour, followed at a cautious distance. She had left a trail of bright red splashes on the clean floor. At the fire-exit door she turned. "Give my love to your sister. I only wanted to help her. You must believe that."

"But you didn't give her any choice," said Daniel, with sudden indignation. "You'd no right."

"Can you honestly look me in the eye and say you prefer her the way she was?" said Mrs Ivory in her kindest voice.

Daniel thought of the old Louie, with her mood swings and tantrums and days of deepest gloom. It was her personality, and without it she was nothing. He held her gaze firmly. "I want her back the way she was."

Mrs Ivory acknowledged this with a sideways dip of her head. "Don't think too badly of me when I'm gone," she said.

Daniel felt a sudden chill at the finality of her words. She was standing very close to the balcony edge and for a moment he thought she was going to throw herself over on to the tiles below. But instead she produced her key ring from her pocket and began working away at the keys with shaking fingers, trying to detach one from the other. "I don't think I'm going to be welcome around here any more," she said, with a crooked smile. "And I've really no desire to spend any time in prison. So…" she shrugged. "I think it's best if I just… disappear."

"You can't just disappear. Not on an island," said Daniel. "And where's Helen? What have you done with her?"

"You want Helen; you find her," she said. "Here's the key – all you've got to do is find the lock."

She seemed to be holding it out to him, but as he took a step towards her she tossed it over the balcony, high into the air. He watched its inevitable trajectory, as it rose and then fell into the deep end of the pool, making a neat splash before sinking gracefully to the bottom. And when he looked up the fire-exit door was swinging open. She was gone.

39

IT TOOK DANIEL no more than a second to decide what to do. Taking the stairs three at a time, he skittered to the poolside, struggling out of his jacket and scuffing off his trainers. He threw himself at the water in the clumsiest dive he'd ever done, feeling the drag of the trapped air in his jeans as he clawed his way downwards. His lungs felt ready to collapse when at last he burst back on to the bright surface with the key clutched in his hand.

Water streamed from his hair and clothes as he ran out through the changing rooms and splashed along flooded corridors, towards the admin block. Mrs Ivory didn't realise that he knew all too well where to find the crucial lock. He hoped this tiny grain of good fortune would save valuable time, though his mind veered away from just what he might be too late for.

As he reached the corridor of offices and storerooms, he could hear a furious thumping noise of someone kicking at a door and he realised he was shaking with relief. "Helen," he called, his voice emerging as a croak. "Are you all right?"

"Daniel!" came the reply. "Yes. No. I'm locked in."

"It's OK. I've got the key," he said, snagging it in the lock and almost snapping it in half in his haste to let her out.

The door flew open. Helen had a large swelling above one eyebrow and looked extremely dishevelled. There were wet patches on her jeans, as though she had been sitting or lying on the floor. Around her lay dismembered cardboard boxes, their contents scattered over the floor as though someone had turned the place over in a fury.

"Thank God you came," said Helen weakly. "How did you know I was here?"

"I heard it all. I was in her office when you came in.

I was hiding in the cupboard." Helen looked at him with amazement and admiration. "What happened?" he said.

"She decked me," said Helen. "She bloody decked me. I can't believe I fell for it. She said she'd show me how she got the drugs into the students, and for some insane reason I trusted her. Anyway, she brought me here and showed me where the drinking water refills were stored. Whenever they got a new consignment she'd come in at night and empty a syringe of Compound K into every canister. I was leaning over to see the puncture marks in the plastic and she hit me so hard it knocked me backwards. I smacked my head on one of the shelves." She put her hand up to her hair, wincing as she found a cut, sticky with blood. "I think I must have blacked out for a second or two because when I opened my eyes there was water everywhere and I heard her locking the door then setting off the fire alarm. I swear she only did that to drown out the sound of my shouting."

"She wanted the school empty so she could go round slashing all the water coolers," said Daniel.

"Where is she now?" Helen demanded.

"I don't know. She said she was going to 'disappear'."

"You spoke to her!"

"I caught up with her by the pool."

"Then what? She got away?"

"Well, yes. She had a knife and I thought she might have stabbed you. I decided rescuing you was more important than chasing her."

"Thank you," said Helen humbly. "I am grateful, really. I couldn't have done this without you." Daniel gave a shrug of denial. "Anyway, where can she disappear to? She can't get off the island. The only flight left two hours ago, and the next ferry isn't till four. I'll have the police out looking for her by then."

Helen was already striding towards the lobby, so he followed after her.

Through the sliding doors, slightly fogged with condensation, Daniel could see a small knot of onlookers had gathered on the forecourt. A police car – the same one that Daniel had dodged at The Brow – was just pulling up. Before the officer inside could open the door he was besieged by islanders, eager for information.

"That's good service," said Helen. "I haven't even dialled 999."

Daniel hung back. "The problem is, it's me they're after. Someone set fire to the school pavilion. They think it was me, and I can't prove it wasn't."

"But I can." A guilty blush bloomed on Helen's cheeks. "Because it was me."

Daniel gaped like a fish on a slab. "You never…" he spluttered.

"It wasn't deliberate!" she protested. "I knocked a candle over – how was I to know there'd be patches of spilt petrol on the floor? The whole thing went up. I was lucky to get out."

"But what were you doing in there in the first place?"

"When I sneaked back on to the island I didn't have anywhere to stay. I couldn't very well go knocking on doors, saying 'Hello, it's me, the runaway music teacher everyone's been talking about, can you put me up for a few days?' So I hid in the groundsman's store in the pavilion. But I had a little accident with the candle."

"So after the fire, let me guess – you spent that first night in the ruined chapel at Ingle?"

"Correct. And that was fine, apart from the bats and the spiders and a whacking great hole in the roof." She shot him a sidelong glance. "And the fact that it was already being used as a love nest…"

Daniel ignored this remark. He was thinking of what lay ahead, beyond the double doors – the unwelcome attention, the endless questions, the whole torrent of words – and wishing he could be anywhere else.

As if sensing his discomfort, Helen gave his shoulder a reassuring squeeze. "Come on, mate," she said, "deep breath. I've got a feeling this is going to take some explaining."

40

DANIEL SAT SHIVERING in the interview room in the tiny police station in Port Julian, a pool of water forming around his shoeless feet. Someone had been sent to fetch him some dry clothes, but the only thing they had been able to find was a spare police uniform, which he had turned down. Too weird, he decided, even by today's standards. He'd answered all their questions, corroborating Helen's account of everything that had passed between her and Mrs Ivory in the headteacher's study, and describing the sabotaging of the water coolers. The only detail he omitted was sending the fake email, which he chose to keep to himself. Helen had admitted to accidentally setting fire to the groundsman's hut, but this incident was so dwarfed by more recent drama that it was barely followed up.

Daniel's mum had been present for the entire interview, listening in astonishment as the story unfolded. Occasionally she murmured expressions of dismay, but he was glad to have her there. There was an awkward moment when Helen mentioned 'borrowing' Mrs Milman's name in order to get back on to the island without being stopped. Under normal circumstances his mum would have been furious, but all her anxieties were focused on Louie and the possible effects of Compound K.

"I brought you here because I thought it was safe," her mum wailed. "And look what's happened."

"Louie's only just started taking it," Daniel pointed out. "Some of the students at Stape have been on it for five years." He was thinking of Ramsay.

"I feel totally fine," said Louie placidly.

"What happens now? What are you going to tell the rest of the parents?" Daniel and Louie's mum asked the police officer.

"That's something for the Chief Medical Officer and the school governors to decide," he replied. "I expect they'll want to call a public meeting. Our priority is to try and apprehend Mrs Ivory, so she can answer our questions."

The events of the morning had rocked his mum more than Daniel had anticipated. He'd imagined that any kind of bad news would send her deeper into her depression, but instead it had woken her up as if from a long sleep.

As soon as they got back to The Brow she had run him a hot bath, and when he came down again, clean and warm, there was a welcoming fire burning and pizzas cooking in the oven. Mum had her arms around Louie, and as Daniel walked in, she beckoned him to join them, so that they were crushed in a tight three-way hug. Last time she'd held them like that, he thought, she'd been taller than him: now he towered over her. He could hear her sniffs and gulps, but then Chet came whisking in, and immediately tried to get in on the act, forcing his wet nose into the gaps between them. Somehow it broke the spell and they all laughed.

When they were sitting down, eating, their mum suddenly laid down her knife and fork and said, "I'm so, so sorry."

Daniel and Louie looked up in surprise. "What for?" asked Louie, her mouth full of pizza.

"For everything that's gone wrong. I've let you down in every kind of way since Dad left. I feel so guilty." Daniel made murmurings of denial, but she cut him off. "I've been so wrapped up in my own unhappiness I haven't looked after you."

"We've caused you a lot of grief too," said Louie. "So it's partly our fault."

"No it isn't," she insisted. "I'm the parent. I'm supposed to deal with your problems, not the other way round. I thought coming here would make everything all right, but running away never solves anything. You just end up with all the same old problems you brought with you, plus a bunch of new ones."

"Do you mean you want us to go back to London early?" Daniel asked. There was a tightness in his chest – an iron band squeezing his ribs.

"I think we should. I want to get Louie checked out by a specialist, to make sure her health hasn't been damaged by this drug, and I want to get you both back into proper education before it's too late. I haven't exactly made a success of the home-schooling experiment, have I?"

"It's not too late to start," said Daniel. "We've just been skiving."

His mum shook her head. "You need proper teachers. I'm not up to it."

"But I thought the London house was let for six months. Where would we live?" asked Louie.

"The tenants were a bit shaken up by the burglary and they want to go back to the States early. The rent is all paid up, but they're going home before Christmas."

Daniel sagged in his seat.

"Do you like it here?" his mum asked gently.

His shoulders twitched. "There's a girl…"

"Ah. Well, distance is no barrier these days with email and stuff. And there's an airport here. She can come and stay. Show her London."

"Her parents would never let her. They don't even let me see her here. We have to meet in secret."

"Why's that?"

"Because her dad thinks I'm a dangerous criminal. He's some kind of lawyer – he found out about my record."

Across the table Louie had gone very still.

Mum put her head in her hands. "Oh, Daniel, I'm so sorry."

"Maybe he'll think differently when he finds out what you've done here," said Louie. "You'll be a local hero. They'll probably rename Port Julian after you."

"I don't think so."

"Look," said their mum, "all I can say is I promise

it won't be like it was. I won't be like I was. I'll be strong, and in charge, and when you have problems I'll deal with them like parents are supposed to."

And she reached across the table and gripped Daniel's hand.

41

TRUE TO HER word, Mrs Ivory disappeared.

Just after her encounter with Daniel at the poolside she'd been seen by the caretaker driving out of the school at some speed. Thanks to Helen, border officials put on alert by the local police reported that she had made no attempt to leave either from Darrow airfield or the ferry terminal at Port Julian. But they were looking out for her black Ford Focus. They wouldn't have paid much attention to Kenny in his white van, making the crossing to Plymouth to pick up a new mower. Even if he did look a little more nervous and twitchy than usual.

Then, on the afternoon of the following day, a woman walking her dog came across Mrs Ivory's car, abandoned on Filey Point, a remote promontory on the north of the island, where the sea plucked greedily at the rocky cliffs below. The key was in the ignition and her handbag was on the seat. A lifeboat was launched from Port Julian to search offshore, more perhaps from a sense of duty than with any real hope of success. Those who knew about tides maintained that nothing lost off Filey Point would ever wash up on Wragge.

This latest development added to the toxic mixture of rumour, speculation and half-truth that was rippling around the island. A notice had been pasted on the main doors of the school advising parents and pupils that it would remain closed for the rest of the week. In the meantime, the caretaker and Kenny aired the classrooms, ripped up the ruined carpet and tried to repair the water damage. But students and parents, bewildered by the loss of Mrs Ivory and troubled by rumours of drugs, continued to congregate around the building.

The morning after the discovery on Filey Point, a lone bouquet of lilies appeared at the entrance to the school, and by evening the driveway was a carpet of flowers – long-stemmed roses in cellophane, yellow chrysanthemums tied with satin ribbon, carnations, freesias and lilies. Whatever Mrs Ivory had done, it seemed there were still plenty of people on the island who admired and mourned her.

Helen brought the news to The Brow. She had overheard it in Port Julian, where she had been working in the library, finishing her account of the scandal to email to her editor.

"How awful. What a desperate way to go," said Mum, lowering her voice, with a mother's instinct to protect her children from anything unpleasant. But Louie had already overheard.

"I don't believe it," she said firmly. "Mrs Ivory would never commit suicide. She said it was as bad as murder. If she was the sort of person to commit suicide she'd have done it when Hilly died. Not now."

"You can't really trust what she said," was Helen's reply. "She was quite a skilful liar."

"Didn't she leave a note?" Louie wanted to know.

"Who for?" said Helen. They digested this sobering thought in silence.

Daniel noticed that Helen seemed quite shaken by this turn of events. He wondered whether it was dismay at Mrs Ivory's sad and lonely end, or the thought of all the evidence and unanswered questions now lost to the waves.

The news of Mrs Ivory's disappearance wasn't Helen's only bombshell. "The paper won't run the story," she said flatly.

"But they sent you here to investigate it in the first place," said Daniel.

"My editor did. I emailed him a draft and he ran it past the libel lawyers and they said, no way. We're only a small independent paper and Narveng is a massive multinational company. If we print anything about them which we can't prove in court they will sue us into oblivion."

"But once they realise how much we know, how could they deny it?"

Helen shook her head. "My editor sent Narveng's head of communications a copy of my piece, asking if they had any comment to add. Within an hour they'd applied for a court injunction and couriered round a forty-page document, denying any involvement in an experiment, and threatening legal action if we published anything that even *hinted* that Narveng had ever done anything illegal or unethical."

"Mrs Ivory admitted it all. We were both witnesses. Doesn't that count?"

"Sadly, no. Without hard physical evidence, we're just like a couple of drunks on a street corner trying to persuade passers-by that Elvis is still alive."

"Couldn't you try one of the bigger papers?" Daniel's mum suggested. "They're used to taking on big corporations."

"They all say the same thing: bring us the evidence."

Daniel sat quietly, looking out into the garden. Two squirrels were playing chase in the oak tree, tearing around the trunk as though pulled on invisible wire. The last few dead leaves, like flakes of beaten copper, rattled on the bare branches.

He remembered Mrs Ivory's words: *If you run this story, and turn the island into a media circus, it will destroy this community.* There would be a stampede of journalists, photographers, camera crews and documentary makers pouring on to the island – outsiders with no respect for local ways. The people would be portrayed as backward, in-bred bumpkins and Wragge would become famous, not for its beautiful scenery or any of the things that made it special, but as a byword for scandal, secrecy and abuse of children. He could see the headlines: SUICIDE HEAD IN SCHOOL DRUG SHOCKER. TOXIC TEENS IN HAPPY-PILL HORROR. And who would benefit? The newspaper that sold a few hundred extra copies? Its readers, briefly entertained over their morning tea? Helen Swift, making her name as an investigative journalist?

On the other hand, if Narveng succeeded in suppressing the story, wasn't that just another example of the rich and powerful throwing their weight around like a playground bully to intimidate the poor and weak? Maybe the Stape students would be entitled to compensation from Narveng. Maybe in the future, they would need it. Could he really sit back and let Narveng profit from this dangerous experiment?

He could hear his mum's and Helen's voices flowing on as he wrestled with these conflicting ideas. A terrible weariness stole over him and he wished he could just hide away and let events take their course without making a decision. But doing nothing *was* making a decision. He tuned back in to the conversation as Helen was saying, "If only a sample of the drug had survived. Or just one document that incriminated Narveng. But I don't have either."

Daniel stood up and walked to the larder, his limbs feeling heavy and reluctant. On the middle shelf stood ten innocuous-looking bottles of Diet Coke arranged in formation as though for a game of skittles. He took one and put it on the table in front of Helen, squeezing it slightly in the process so that a fine brown jet, like cotton thread, spurted from a puncture mark in the neck.

"But I do," he said, enjoying her open-mouthed astonishment. "I've got both."

42

D ANIEL AND LOUIE followed the procession of flickering lights up the hill towards Filey Point. It was a freezing cloudless night and the moon was a chip of ice in the sky above them. They hadn't seen a crowd like this since the 4th of October fireworks, which seemed a lifetime ago. Then the atmosphere had been festive, the air filled with piped music and barbecue smoke; now it was sombre and the only sound was the crunch of feet on the stony path.

Daniel didn't have much appetite for this cliff-top vigil. And besides, until Mrs Ivory's body was found he would always harbour a faint suspicion that she wasn't dead at all, but out there somewhere, watching. It was the thought that he might see Ramsay there that persuaded him to make the trek. Louie seemed eager to attend for reasons of her own.

Unbelievable turnout, Daniel thought as he and Louie came to the bottom of Filey Hill. Considering what Mrs Ivory had actually done. Most of those milling around with candles in jam jars were teenagers, students from Stape High. *It must be the drug that's making them so forgiving,* he decided. *When it finally wears off they'll start to feel angry.*

The front of the procession had reached the top of Filey Point, and stood in a loose semi-circle waiting for the tail to catch up. No one was quite sure whether they were supposed to be staring out to sea, or watching the column of lights snaking up the hill towards them. Once the last stragglers had arrived, there was an awkward moment as it became clear that the student organisers hadn't really planned what to do next. People waited placidly for something to happen. They looked to Daniel more like a group of carol singers than a group of mourners standing around with their lanterns, but no one led the singing, so nobody sang.

At last, somebody stepped forward and placed their jam-jar candle on the ground in the spot where the car had been found, and stepped back again. There was a general murmur of approval and gradually, one and two at a time, the rest of the congregation did the same until there was a blazing circle of light at their feet. Those furthest from the circle began to break away and move back down the hill, but then stopped, realising that it was now impossible to see the path. People started to go back to fetch their candles, hesitating over whether it was correct protocol to take the nearest one, or to try to locate the one they had originally brought. They got in each other's way, singeing coat cuffs and kicking over jam jars in the confusion. Daniel scanned the faces, trying to pick out Ramsay, and noticed that nobody had shed so much as a tear. Which, he supposed, was precisely what Mrs Ivory would have wanted.

*

Ramsay had stopped to retie her shoelace and when she stood up he was there. The memory of their last meeting, when he'd climbed in her bedroom window, hovered between them.

"I hoped I'd find you here," he said. "Are you OK?"

Of all the shocks and revelations that had landed one after another since the evacuation of the school, Daniel leaving had hit her harder than any. The betrayal by Mrs Ivory, the drugging, the suicide, were disasters shared by the whole community; the departure of Daniel she would bear alone.

"Have you come to say goodbye?" Her eyes shone in the candlelight.

"How do you know we're going?" They began to walk down the path together, using her candle as a guide.

"Someone saw your mum in the post office filling in a form to have the mail re-directed. They mentioned it to someone, who mentioned it to someone else…"

"Right," said Daniel. "Of course."

"You'll be glad to get away from this crazy place," she said, lightly. "Back to civilisation."

"No I won't," he insisted. "I even rang up the freezing works and the furniture warehouse to see if they had any jobs so I could stay."

"Uh-huh. So did you get a job?"

"I wasn't being very realistic."

"So what are you actually going to do?"

"Sixth form, in London. I've got loads to catch up. And then university if anywhere'll have me."

"You've got it all planned." She could see his future unrolling without her somewhere far away.

"Not really. I don't even know what subjects I'm going to do. The only bit I'm sure about is going to university. You could go too. We could go to the same one." Ramsay laughed at this preposterous idea. "I mean it. Then we could see each other every day if we wanted."

"That's ages away. We won't even know each other by then."

There was a silence as they both considered what they

had been doing two years ago. "OK it is ages," he conceded. "But we can email and phone and stuff. I wouldn't forget you in two years. I won't forget you in ten."

She smiled, flattered. Somehow his arm had got around her shoulders, and they walked on like this until they reached the village. A number of cars were parked in the square, waiting to give lifts. Ramsay pointed out her parents standing beside their Land Rover deep in conversation with Fay and Louie, who seemed to be doing most of the talking.

"I wonder what she's saying," said Daniel uneasily.

"She looks very pale," said Ramsay, as Louie approached.

"I just did it," said Louie quietly. "And it wasn't so difficult really."

Daniel was staring at his sister in disbelief. "You didn't say anything about—"

"I told them the truth. I should have told the truth from the start. But I was too weak and scared."

"Louie, don't. It's done and forgotten. Don't drag it up."

"It's not forgotten. And it never will be all the time we keep it a secret." She turned to Ramsay. "Daniel never lit the fire that killed that man. I did. It was an accident, but he took the blame because he thought I wouldn't be able to cope with police and questions and court, and I might get put in care."

"It doesn't matter now," Daniel protested, but she was unstoppable.

"And he was right. I wouldn't have coped; I would have killed myself. So he went to that place, Lissmore, instead and pretended that it was OK, even though we knew it wasn't. We knew it was awful, but we never talked about it, even after he came out, because I was so ashamed that I'd let him lie to everyone, and Mum was so ashamed that she'd let Daniel sacrifice himself. If she'd been stronger, she'd have stopped him. But once he'd told the police, it was like an express train – there was no way of getting off."

"I wish you'd told me," said Ramsay.

"I couldn't say what really happened, but I didn't

want to lie to you either. So it was best to say nothing. The very first time we met you told me that you can't have a secret on Wragge."

"That's what I always thought. But it took an outsider to uncover the biggest secret of all," said Ramsay.

43

TWO WEEKS LATER the dented estate car sat on the quayside at Port Julian waiting for the incoming ferry to unload.

As before, Daniel was in the back seat, being trampled and breathed on and slobbered over by Chet, while Louie sat in front, with squashable luggage tucked around her feet. There was slightly more space this time, as they had left some boxes of belongings behind at The Brow as a sort of guarantee that they would return. Easter was mentioned by Mum in that non-committal way that was supposed to offer hope without being a promise. Daniel had it fixed in his mind as a firm date.

Louie had accepted the decision to leave quite calmly when it was first discussed, but on the morning of their departure she had cried a storm of tears, and raged against the unfairness of things – just like the old Louie.

At last the ramp was lowered and cars rolled down on to the dockside, a long queue forming at the barrier. Without waiting for clearance, the occupants of a silver van began to unload camera and sound equipment, preparing for an outside broadcast. Other drivers and passengers abandoned their vehicles and strolled around, chatting, smoking and complaining about their dead mobile phones. They all seemed to know each other, as members of the same profession often do. One of them, a man with a leathery complexion tracked by purple veins, driven to fury by the lack of signal, gave up and chucked his phone into the harbour, to general laughter and applause.

Ramsay paid her pound and pushed past the turnstile into the lighthouse at the eastern tip of Port Julian. She climbed up the narrow spiral staircase until she emerged on to the platform in a buffeting gale. The noise was tremendous after the quiet interior of the tower – wind, stinging spray and the scream of gulls, and far below the sea like a sheet of crumpled metal.

The ferry had left the calm waters of the harbour and was riding the whitecaps in the bay. She and Daniel had said their goodbyes the day before, but when she'd woken up this morning she felt that she had to watch the boat until it was out of sight.

"Don't think of it as two years," he'd said. "I'll come back and see you at Easter. That's only…" he screwed up his face as he did the sum, and then his face stretched into a stunned smile, "…119 days!"

She could see the cars on the deck, tiny coloured bricks, neatly spaced. Somewhere in one of them Chet would be chewing the upholstery, or forcing his snout through a gap in the windows, while in the passenger lounge Daniel would be sleeping or playing cards or maybe thinking of her.

She watched the ferry's creeping progress towards the horizon, until it was swallowed up by the milky haze, and then, putting her hands up to her face, she found it was wet with tears. Instead of trying to blink them away, she let them fall from a vast reservoir deep inside her. She put her hand in her pocket for a tissue and pulled out instead a paper bag of Leaf. For a moment she looked at the limp withered shreds in surprise, before scattering them over the balcony to stream away into the wind.